Sail Away Land

Sail Away Land

Ben Pester

GRANTA

Granta Publications, 12 Addison Avenue, London W11 4QR

First published in Great Britain by Granta Books, 2026

'Around the time of my promotion' was first published in *The London Magazine*; 'The Durhams' was first published in *Granta*; 'Sail Away Land' (as 'Downsizer') and 'square / recess / moon' were first published in *Exacting Clam*; 'Catmint' was first published in *Hotel*; 'You and me, and Russel Palomet' was first published in *Inque*; 'The door in the back of Simon's head' was first published in *Port*; 'A conversation near a window' was first published in *Mercurius*; and 'Exit interview for a Valued Colleague' was first published in *Lunate*.

A CIP catalogue record for this book is available from the British Library.

1 3 5 7 9 10 8 6 4 2

ISBN 978 1 80351 429 1
eISBN 978 1 80351 430 7

Typeset in Bembo by Iram Allam
Printed and bound by CPI Group (UK) Ltd, Croydon, CR0 4YY

The manufacturer's authorised representative in the EU for product safety is BGC Sustainability & Compliance, 7 avenue du Général Leclerc, 75014 Paris, France (gpsr@baldwinglobalconsulting.com)

www.granta.com

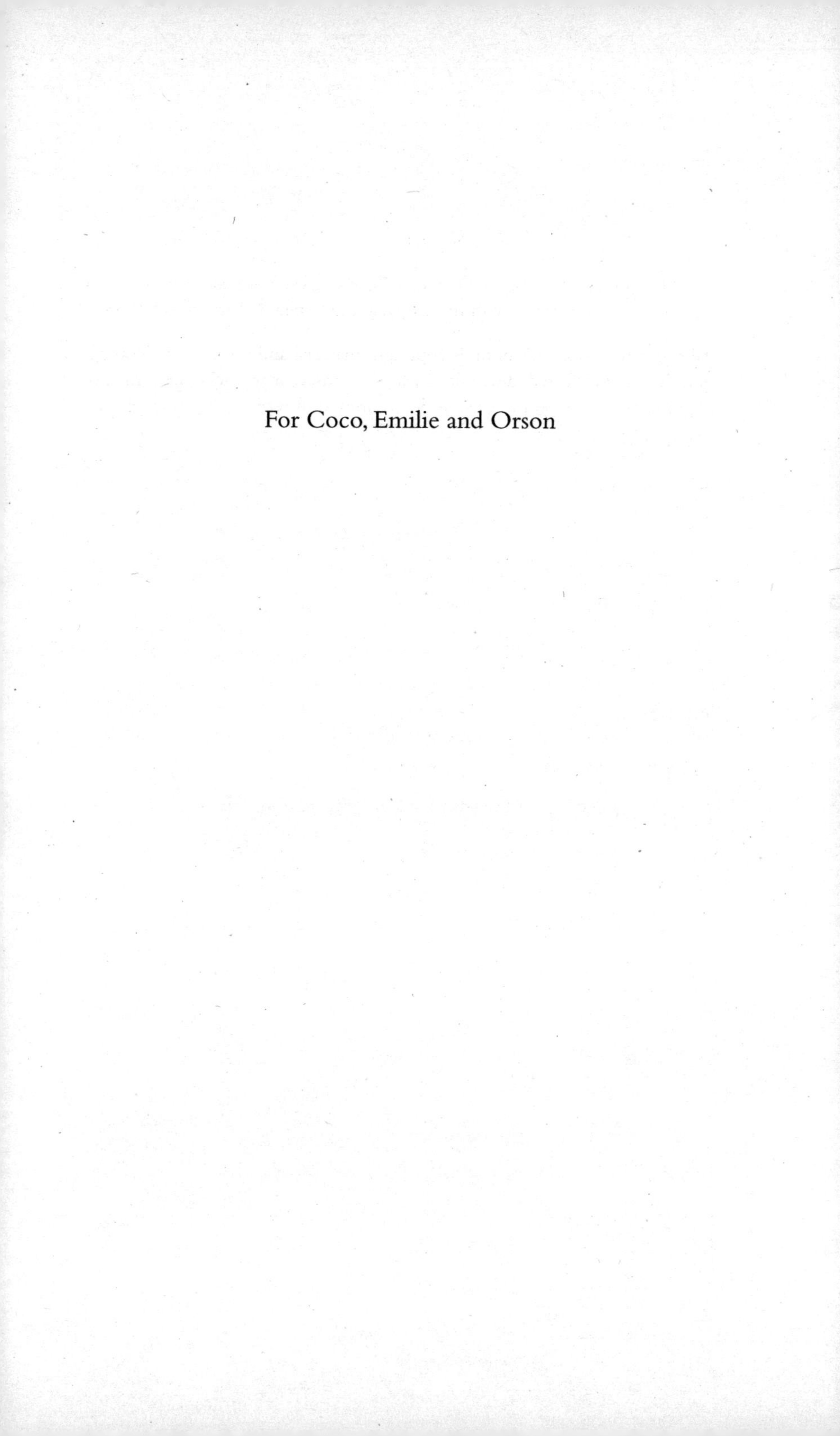

For Coco, Emilie and Orson

Contents

Around the time of my promotion   1

An improvement in the light   16

Grass laminate   19

The Durhams   28

A goshawk   45

Celia in the mist   65

Sail Away Land   67

Catmint   83

Sonic Gold   103

square / recess / moon   119

The people in the kitchen   132

You and me, and Russel Palomet   142

The door in the back of Simon's head   165

A conversation near a window   167

Exit interview for a Valued Colleague   177

Around the time of my promotion

Someone has just asked me a question – they are politely waiting for my answer. There is a plant in a pot in the area behind them. There's a recess in the wall with a lamp in it. There is a clean jug of water, and the smell of lemons. The legs of the chairs and the tables are round and thin-looking. Mid-century, is that right? Modern? They have just finished asking it, this question.

The whole situation reminds me of the time I was given a promotion. It was a long time ago, my promotion. The promotion was preceded by an annual review. I was asked how I felt I had performed.

This now is a different kind of question. I have not been asked about my performance, but the room is the same type of room. I am absorbed by the colour of the carpet. I am worried about what might come out of me when I speak, but I am speaking. I am speaking but not yet answering the question.

I live by the sea, and I have this morning traced my favourite path along the shingle, pushing my heels between the stones, looking at the colour of the sea and the colour of the sky, like a municipal door in a municipal door frame.

I have begun veering towards a subject area with the potential to be the beginnings of an answer to the question I have been asked.

My voice sounds dry. Living by the sea has done this to me. The salt air, the dirt on the stones, the fibred wind. I'm more or less croaking. The question is repeated with a smile, I must not have understood. I speak again.

Not long after you left, we started sending you postcards of the castle. I was the first to do it. I had found a postcard by accident, hidden in a paper bag that I think was from our first ever visit to the castle, when we first moved to this town.

The castle was a ruin, of course. I remember having a sense of disappointment on that first visit, that there was no roof, and no real rooms to frolic around in, no hallways to charge along.

The gift shop had been the only comfort against the castle's slighted form. A place that represented what a castle was supposed to be. A warm room filled with wooden swords, sweet-fragranced stationery, stuffed toy lions. I had wanted a suit of armour made out of that shimmering clacking gold plastic, complete with paladin's cape and sword, but they cost way too much money. Instead, we always bought postcards and were dutifully made to sit down and write them to members of the family. To Grandma, to Gran and Grandad, to Uncle Martin. But this one had never been sent – it had remained in its paper bag with candy-pink stripes.

I found it in the drawer of doom, down under the crusted layers of bills and yearly reports. I slipped it out of its crunchy paper bag, and I thought of you.

As soon as the idea came to me, I wrote my message and copied out the address you had scrawled on the back of an envelope for us. My writing was very messy – very rushed. I did not manage to say everything I wanted to say.

The next morning, on the way to school, I lagged behind the family shoal so I could slip it into the postbox without being seen. As I heard it hit the other letters inside, I felt a surge of quite painful happiness. I thought about its impact a lot that day. I wondered what you would do. I had literally no idea which way things would play out.

The next day, there was a trouble I had not accounted for. I was called downstairs by my mother. I was convinced I was about to get quizzed about my postcard, and its contents. I felt suddenly as though I had done something very wrong – there was no doubt that I had broken the unspoken rules of what could be said and what could not be said about your departure. I had been too direct. When I saw my mother's face, I became overwhelmed by the thought that I had hurt her. I had gone behind her back, expressed my sadness to you, and in so doing weakened and insulted her as a parent. I felt like a traitor.

In fact, it was not that. But it was, in that particular moment, much more serious – much more tangibly bad. It turned out that I had used the last stamp. Mum was angry and desperate because she needed the stamp to send a cheque to pay a bill that was weeks overdue. There was hell that morning. There was no time to buy another stamp, there was no money for another stamp. We were on pennies for beans already, but I didn't answer her question – where is the stamp? I was meant to know that Direct Debits were not possible for us. I could not explain what I had used the stamp for, so I just apologised and said over and over again that it wasn't my brother's fault or my sister's fault, it was probably my fault, but I didn't know what I had done with it. I didn't know where it was, I said, and we went on looking pointlessly around the house, wasting more and more time and generating more and more rage, late for everything, with the toast burnt and so on. A classic hell morning.

In my postcard, of course, I wrote that you should come back. I knew it was a forbidden thing to say. I said that it would be better if we were all together – I tried to assemble an argument that made it clear. I said I could tell that you were not happy.

In sending this and subsequent postcards, I hoped you would see that the separation was tearing me apart, actually. Even though I had said it was fine – and continued to say it was fine when we spoke on the phone, and when I was asked at school, and by uncles and by friends of the family, to all of them I said it was fine. I was happy. I nodded when I was asked if I understood that it had been the only way. I let them say how grown-up I was for being fine.

In the postcard, I tried to point out what I hoped you knew: that it would be obvious to you that it was in fact the very worst thing in the world.

I missed you. I missed hearing you and smelling the tobacco on your breath when you kissed me goodnight. Come back, it said, just come back.

The question I have been asked is still in the air. The plant is still there somewhere. I have not answered it. I have not engaged with the subject at all, and while they wait, someone is pouring water, so slowly, it feels like a test. The sound of pouring water is a test – the test is, can I resist becoming a liquid? I should be clear: I am speaking, but not managing to answer the question. My voice is very crunchy. They are looking at me, they are peering at me, I do not seem to realise how momentous this is. The carpet beneath all our feet is the colour they tell me dominates the colour of space. A kind of peach beige brown sick colour, but of course with infinite depth, with a darkness that really draws all of this in – that inevitably will dominate all colour and all of time. I go again.

Later that day, when I was alone with my brother and sister, I confessed that it was me who took the stamp. I told them why and what I had done with it. I felt that they deserved an explanation. They were hugely embarrassed at having our common sadness suddenly out in the open, as we sat at the table, without any warning, and us still in our school uniforms eating chips and with the evening TV ahead of us, but they grudgingly approved of what I had done. David asked if we could get some more stamps. Susan agreed. We want to write to him too, she said.

Careful not to make too much of a dent in the precious money bowl that was hidden in our mother's bedroom, we took enough coppers to pay for a book of second-class stamps. The postcards themselves I shoplifted from stands outside the various gift shops in town as I walked home from school. I took only the cheapest, most faded pictures of the castle. I tried to get ones nobody was ever likely to buy now anyway, and yet also ones that my brother and sister would like and be happy with.

I never told them that the postcards were stolen, and they didn't ask.

So we sent you only the castle, different aspects of its ruined shape. It became our thing. We sent you pictures framed by an archer's slit, through which you could see broken stones of the old keep walls. We sent you the Elizabethan residences and the meadow on the other side. In an etching of the waters that once surrounded the outer wall, the artist had imagined a boat with two people on the lake, dwarfed by the scale and the romance of the portcullis. They have no oars or fishing lines. They are sitting in the boat, looking directly at one another.

We went on with the postcards for a few weeks, during which time our expectation swelled to engulf every ritual of our days. Over our dinners, we asked and answered questions about how many days it had been. We huddled in the bedroom I shared with David. Susan would come in and tell us what she wanted to write to you. I want to tell him, she said, that we are all sick without him.

She said she would describe symptoms of a terrible illness, which made your skin turn grey and spongy, and if you got it snagged on anything, your skin could come off in chunks.

David said that he just wanted to say that he really liked you. And he wanted to tell you that you are cool.

I went on with my reserved sentences, stating simply how much better it would be if we were together, and still hoping that the subtext would clearly be of jumpers, tobacco on your breath, and being held in the air like I weighed nothing at all.

It came to feel impossible that the project would fail. We considered the postcards, and their persuasiveness, as a single irresistible application of pressure. Each card was a small breath of air, breathed with our sighs into the postbox in the wall at the corner of School Lane. The bubble membrane holding our promises and our broken hearts would soon give way, and would explode and shock you, bursting this bad dream you were in, so you could come home.

When we saw you at weekends, or spoke on the phone on Thursday evenings, we did not mention the postcards. You did not acknowledge that we had sent them to you.

One Thursday, your voice was especially weak, and sounded thin. You were pitifully sad. When I asked why, you told me it was because you had been forced to give up smoking. You could no longer afford tobacco, you said.

I advocated vehemently that if you wanted to smoke, then you should smoke. What was the point in being healthy if you were so sad? I said I would speak to Mum and say we didn't need the money that you would normally send us — at least to the value of the tobacco. Which of course I never actually did. We desperately needed every single penny, and, as you knew, a lot more besides.

We kept sending the postcards. The more you didn't acknowledge it was happening, the more we sent.

Eventually, Mum had to take us to one side and explain things. She said that sometimes we had to accept that things were over, and we had to let them go. She told us that even though we might think we were doing something very kind, it could in fact be quite painful for the other person.

I remember the specific rage I felt because she would not say what she was talking about. Because she would not just come out and say it was the postcards — that they were embarrassing you. They were like poison to you.

And then, as if it was not connected to what she had just been saying, Mum told us that you were not feeling well and wouldn't be able to see us, or talk on the phone, for at least a couple of months, maybe more. She told us not to worry. And then she told us that she had found a ten-pound note buried in her purse. Magic money! That was its name when this happened, and she would take us for a nice lunch out somewhere.

This conversation with Mum came back to me years later when I was in a meeting with my line manager and the head of HR. They had asked me a question.

This was when I worked as an administrator for the marketing 'team' – a team which consisted of my line manager and me. The head of HR was telling me that although we were a small company, it was possible to see a way forward if you had the right attitude, to progress to where you wanted to be. They were telling me that I was to receive a modest pay increase, and they wanted me to stay on at the company after the end of my temporary contract.

'We have loved working with you so much,' my manager told me. 'We do have to really knuckle down and bring in some money, but it would be wonderful to have you here. I think you can really help us do it!'

The way she looked at me, with big, smiling eyes, giving me this news that I had been hoping for for weeks, I suddenly wanted to get out of that office as fast as I could. I wanted to run away and never talk to them again.

There was a very long pause in the room, before the HR manager (who was also the chief financial officer and office manager) said, 'Are you able to make a decision fairly quickly? Because we would like to have a little celebration later!'

I sat there in that office. It was the easiest job I ever had. I looked at the plant in the corner of the room. I looked at the sad little kettle on the work surface. I looked at the jar of biscuits that was smeared with crumbs and fat on the inside. I could not speak.

My mouth was filled, at that moment, with the flavour of the ink on the postcards that I sent you. And then there was an actual post card in my mouth. It had somehow been lodged in my stomach somewhere.

Both my line manager and the head of HR looked appalled as I tried to speak, but instead of speaking, I started gagging and my first postcard to you fell out, creased and badly balled up, covered in cords of clear spit. It landed on the coffee table. We all stared down at the postcard. The head of HR made a noise in her throat like a little donkey.

Eventually you moved into a new place. I felt a lurch of humiliation and hope when I saw my postcard there in your cold kitchen, shoved in with a load of other letters in a big Real McCoy's box in the corner. Salt and vinegar flavour, the McCoy's that had once been in the box had been. Now all the crisps were gone, and one of my postcards was in there with confidential papers from your work and a dusty wooden statue of a heron. Just one, I saw, but it had the weight of all of them, of all the stones of a castle. It was the first one I ever sent. It featured several red-white-and-gold flags flying from different towers in the castle ruin. Even covered in my spit, unfurling on the smoked glass table in the office in my promotion meeting, those blazing flags managed to fill me with shitty old hope.

I picked up the postcard and held it in my hands while the head of HR and my line manager asked me if I was all right, and fetched me some water, and opened a window and asked again and again if I was all right, and why had I eaten a postcard?

I couldn't answer, I barely managed to explain to them that I had lacerations, or what felt like lacerations, inside my throat from ejecting the postcard. The writing on the postcard, though streaked and smudged, was still clear. It had been written in fountain pen and streaked where my clumsy left hand had brushed over the wet ink.

The postcard told you a story about how David had thrown himself down an iced slope on the way home from school. He said he wanted to try to skid down the hill on the ice, but, I wrote, I think he was just incredibly sad. We think he is doing these things to get attention. Maybe when you see us at the weekend, you could give him a little bit of confidence. Or maybe we could spend longer with you on your own, without anyone else there. I'm worried about Susan too, but I think that might be trickier to solve.

I explained my motivation for writing the postcard to my line manager and the head of HR. My line manager gave me some lemon tea with honey in.

For your throat, she said. She had creased, sad eyes.

We laughed about how it was possible that I had eaten a postcard. I let them go on thinking that it had been a crazy sleepwalking-type event. I must have risen up in the night and swallowed it whole, I said.

If you're having these painful memories about your father, my line manager said, it's possible you are somnambulating, which does mean sleepwalking, but it can include things like this, I think. Eating and so on. I'm sure – I'm sure it happens, she said.

She had seen a documentary about this sort of thing. She wanted to know if I had seen a witch at the end of my bed. An old crone? she said. A hag?

No, I didn't see anything like that. And, also, I wouldn't use that term, I told her. Hag, or whatever. My grandmother had a stoop. Terrible pain, I told them. She was always in terrible pain, and whenever it was Halloween, she used to hate that image, the image of the hag in every shop, the shadow of the witch. That's a woman with a bad back, she would say. What harm can she do to you?

We sat for a while and looked at the postcard on the table. Of course, I did not try to explain that, when I was a boy, and I noticed this exact postcard in the McCoy's crisps box in the corner of your new kitchen, I secretly climbed down from my seat at your oversized pine table, crossed the room and snatched it up.

With my brother and sister watching me, I took the postcard, tore it into tiny pieces and then dumped it in the bin. Later that night, I had to stand in the living room and tell you that I had no idea why David and Susan were crying, why they were inconsolable. Everything was cold and smelt wrong in that house. There was a lot of batik hanging on the walls, and there were wooden sculptures which were huge and we weren't allowed to touch.

Why are they crying? you wanted to know. But you also had no idea how to force the issue. How could you be so cruel to your brother and sister? you wanted to know, but I just stood there saying, I don't know. I have no idea. And you threatened to not let me see grandma and I told you that I didn't care about seeing her anyway. I said, Fuck grandma, and I was sent to bed, and did not eat dinner.

When the head of HR moved round the table to sit closer to me in my promotion meeting, I thought she was going to hug me, but she only offered a tissue. She gave me a few more minutes to dry my eyes, which I told her were stinging from drinking too much honey and lemon at once with my lacerated throat.

I understand, she said. But actually, you know, you haven't said yes yet.

She placed a hand on my back and I felt a strong wave of nausea and a desperate need to run away. My line manager made a small, desperate noise that told me she really expected an answer right then, in that very second. Do you accept the promotion? She asked me.

Yes, I croaked. Yes please. Another tightly balled postcard emerged from my mouth and we cleaned it up without speaking. Then Tony, the CEO, came down with bottles of champagne, and later we had a steak dinner at Browns.

My partner was glad I finally had a permanent job, but a month or so later the good feeling of my promotion had faded. The flat we shared started to feel cold. Both she and I had taken up smoking again, something we had both stopped a year before.

She was unhappy, she told me. She sat me down and she said, We have reached the end of this.

I think you might be right, I said.

I'm unhappy, she told me. And then I realised that quite a lot of her belongings were no longer in the flat.

I'll stop sending them, I said. I'll stop sending you postcards.

Don't start talking about postcards, she said.

She sounded very sad. It's not like I didn't understand. Things had been stale for a long time. We were smoking so much. We were eating the most awful food, and we were drinking.

Every day, you lie in bed while I get up, she said.

Well, I start later than you.

You lie in bed. You hear me telling you how sick of everything I am. And you lie there.

I really do, I said. I'm sorry. I just lie there, I said. Is it because you don't like the pictures of the castle?

I don't like it when you talk about the castle, she said.

Her voice changed.

I actually asked about a time you feel you exceeded expectations.

I have been asked a question again. It's the same question. A voice reminds me – this is a job interview. Would you like a glass of water?

I was lying there in our messy bed, and I was trying to figure out a way of asking my partner if she loved me still, but without actually asking that because I had promised several times to stop asking that question.

Is it over, then?

I'm so sorry, she said.

Do we still have to go to the party? I asked her. We were meant to be going to a friend's birthday party.

I think you should go on your own.

I am trying to remember an example in my previous role where I exceeded expectations. I do not believe I have ever exceeded expectations, but I am preparing to say that I have. I am preparing to say something devastatingly impressive.

You met her once, I don't know if you remember, but I took her to your house. A different house, not the one you moved into with the box of McCoy's in the corner of the kitchen. A house in a different part of the country. I showed her your photograph albums – pictures of me in shorts, covered in freckles, lookin' out for wasps. David and Susan too. We looked at pictures of my grandma.

She was in pain a lot of the time, I told my partner while we looked at the pictures. My grandma was there in the picture holding a CV, standing in the garden.

She was very beautiful, my partner said, holding the photograph of my grandmother, who was holding you as a baby in her arms. And you were holding your CV.

She was a real bright spark, you said. When she was younger.

We sat in a row, you, me and my partner on your sofa, and looked at all the different pictures in your photo albums. Photos of things I never saw in real time. Like your wedding to your new partner.

I told you then, on the sofa, in a moment of strange generosity, how sorry I was that I had missed your wedding.

You sent a card, you said.

I did, I said.

Of course, in fact, I had done no such thing. I didn't bother to correct the lie in front of my partner, who was by this stage very tired from the travelling, and the obvious tension between you and me.

In my promotion meeting, I picked up the damp postcards and put them away in my pocket. That seemed to be a kind of end to it.

Everyone said they were very glad that I had accepted the promotion, but we did not go out to celebrate. Instead, we carried on working for the usual hours, and then said goodbye and went home. I did not do many of my actual duties that day – instead I read through my new contract, and I read the terms of my new employment, and I wondered if I should have tried to get a more significant pay rise, or extra holiday or something.

My line manager seemed less sure about their decision to promote me since I had vomited postcards out of myself.

At around 4 p.m., she approached me at my desk. Quite tentatively, she said, You know, I hate that phrase old crone too. Old hag, she said. It's a horrible way to talk about someone. My mother has terrible arthritis, and she won't listen to us. She goes out in the cold. I worry about her. People say that word when they see her. Kids on her street, Old Hag, because she is in so much pain, her face, her body, all crooked. It's a terrible way to talk about somebody.

I'm sorry, I said. I meant I was sorry for what happened, but I made sure I could also be sorry to hear that my manager's mother had arthritis.

I worry about her especially in the winter months, she told me.

As my partner and I continued the strange ritual of our break-up conversation, I kept having the urge to throw myself on the floor at her feet, to clutch her and beg her not to leave me. I had the urge to scream for her to stop the process, to reverse it all. To come back to me. But I didn't say anything of course, or throw myself on the floor.

It was actually going to be fine, is what I said. You and I both deserve happiness. We are young, I said. This is absolutely fine. And I will always love you a bit.

Yes, just a small amount, she concurred. Like a residue of it.

Like harmless nuclear waste after it has finished being toxic.

Like just carbon, she said. Dead lifeless carbon that will float in space even when all the light in the universe has been spent, and time winds away in the dark.

We were laughing together by the time I had to leave for the party, but everything was incredibly cold. And I knew that when I came back, I would have to sleep in a different room, and soon she would be gone.

As I stepped out, alone, as we had agreed, and shaking with adrenaline from the fact that I was breaking up with my partner who I did love in a very real way, albeit now with a dead kind of love, I saw something.

What's that? I shouted to my partner. Come and look!

As I emerged out onto the road, I saw a shape in the distance, someone hunched up so that they were very small, coming down the hill towards me. It was a woman; dressed entirely in black, and walking in a painful, lateral kind of way.

Hello, I called out to the shape. Are you all right?

The shape did not answer, but the movement was so skittish, I became worried that whoever it was would slip. Our flat was on one of the steepest hills in town. It was quite hazardous to go walking downhill on a frosty night, even for the sure-footed.

Hello! I called again, quite loudly. I wanted the person to hear me. Can I help you?

All at once, the person seemed to reach out to me, and then let out a sharp cry as she slipped onto her back. It was such a brittle action, I felt sure I had seen something break. I rushed up the hill, calling to my partner, Come and help! Come and help!

She was old – the woman who had fallen. Maybe even in her nineties, her skin was dark and her mouth delirious, her eyes kept rolling back in her head. The pit of her mouth was a colourless space under the streetlights and the moon.

My partner brought out a pillow for under the woman's head and we put blankets over her.

Did you bring your phone out? I asked, but my partner had not.

I'll stay with her, she said.

Yes, good idea, I said. Don't let her go to sleep.

I rushed back to the house while my now former partner remained up the hill, holding the head of the woman. Though she spoke softly, her words carried across the sharp night air. I could hear her saying, Don't worry. Don't worry, but it sounded exactly like she was saying, Don't go, please. I don't want you to sail away.

It's too late. I am saying thank you. I am saying goodbye. I have not answered the question, of course.

An improvement in the light

A few people come here to the village directly from the hospital. Not a single specific hospital, of course, but one of many hospitals that have become known to the individual as 'the Hospital'.

It could be any hospital, any hospital where the end of the ward finishes out of sight, in that quiet darkness. Or they may have been alone in a corner room, awake and exhausted, no longer in St James Infirmary or Central Mids A & E, but now in the Hospital.

They come still with the residue of short breath, or with clouding pain in the kidneys, and we escort them or carry them, in a kind of floating holding method, towards the central communal meeting area. At the heart of the central communal meeting area is a long, cool building with sweet low ceilings and gorgeous windows. There is ample room for anyone who comes here still in pain from before.

One of the new arrivals recently was called Sean (not his real name). First thing he said was his eyes ached like hell. They had ached since he left. He explained to me that it was like the lights were not getting enough power at his end of the ward. The bulbs felt heavy, he said. Slow and thick. There was a sort of pressure on the light, you see, and it pressed on his eyes. As though there was a problem with the power exchange locally, and also a problem with the pressure in the air.

Figures who came to him at his bedside spoke in deep, granular voices. They seemed concerned about him, but were unable to stay. He heard them speaking low, goopy diagnoses. He made no sense at all of their attentions.

Alone at night, the weight of the slow light became worse and worse until he forced himself out of the bed, and walked towards the truer darkness, away from the sturdy corridor of slippers and monitors. He moved towards the unseen limit of the ward, where the boundary had become vague and a cool air promised that the pressure would lift.

As he moved through the limits, the light rolled from his mind like syrup. He felt the air soften and go dark, he heard feathers – light movements, like an owl turning, glancing and lifting again. He made his way quietly through the mist. He was not taunted by the figures, but silently allowed to pass on until he emerged in the village, still aching, in need of help.

I led him, while he spoke, through the long central communal meeting area building, towards not a bed, but a fine armchair in a pool of isolated air. The chair was positioned facing a high window through which came the scent of pines and a swift warm breeze. I gave him some tea. I gave him a cold hat to wear, made of thick, soft cotton, soaked in fresh water to ease the pressure on his eyes.

He continued explaining that he missed his family a great deal. They would not know why he left the ward the way he did. The Hospital people too, who were kind people, would be confused. But his family, yes that was bad. He explained that they would struggle without him, without his contributions of labour, and kindness and maybe teaching, and yet all of these things he had also accepted. You cannot return from the village.

Still, he would have loved to have had one last time with them. To experience them coming into a room while he was dozing, and wake him with an embrace and the questions of how are you feeling and shall we go for a walk then?

We sat in silence for a short time after this. Yes, he confirmed at length, I would have liked that.

I suggested that he might enjoy coming to see me for a cup of tea one day soon. I explained about the ladder I have set up in the garden, where we can say frivolous things and hope we become lighter for it, and the hole a few of us have dug which feels like you are being incubated in an egg if you lie in it. We talked about the possibility of flight. Sean only really committed to having a cup of tea.

He said he was not sure about heights. He remembered a window, long ago, a window where he stood looking down at the night and feeling a long, enduring surge of loneliness.

Grass laminate

It happens beside the water, just next to the bridge. I can hear the sound of other kids playing over across the pond. I can see them at the top of the climbing frame, laughing. Between the swaying branches of the tree, I can see them. If I were with them over there, playing, right now, it would be normal. I would not be out of place. I can imagine it, doing the thing of going round the obstacles without touching the ground. I'm not *so* old. I should be able to stand up and walk over there and play. But of course I cannot stand up.

I almost laugh at the idea. It comes up like a ball that I have to swallow immediately back down. I cannot go over there. I cannot go and play. Laughing at these things too would be a terrible mistake.

I remember, I was with my sister last time I actually played over there. A year ago, maybe. Already too old, but it was Mum insisting, raging. Get out from under my feet please, she said. Go to the park. Get some air. Banging the doors, turning off the television. It seemed so childish and silly of course, the idea of playing, but we went, shaped into younger versions of ourselves by the specific anger she held at that time. We slipped out with the escaping air, the unbearable pressure of a weekend in which our mother was working, trying to get something finished. The town – our part of town – felt so small around us. I think we held hands, maybe as a joke to make her laugh, but maybe we didn't.

I remember, and I don't know.

I want to remember more things – it's hard at the moment, because of what's happening, and also my breathing is not steady, I'm trying to keep it steady.

I do remember that, on that day, it seemed to me my sister felt light in the same way I felt light. In the park. Playing. Just over there.

I can hear the wind in the long grass. The golden sun, my skin raw, the blue sky. The children play louder, like a song.

The boys stand in an arc around me.

The knife is strange. From a kitchen, but not what my mother would call a good working knife. The blade is thin and long. It would be hard to cut onions with it, I know that. I cut the onions and I use a paring knife. This one is wrong. It's for carving meat, maybe. The plastic handle is wrapped in tape. They're talking to me, one of them leading the others. I think they're enjoying watching it, but in an angry way. They're frightened, maybe, of what's happening. There's a taste. I wonder if they can also taste it.

I think of the one with the knife as the main one. This is actually all about him.

His head is small. Under his coat, his body is thin. Weak-looking, if you saw him naked in a photo. But it doesn't matter – strong/weak. It doesn't matter when you're the main one. He is everything. He has all the power in the world.

He must have taped that handle himself at some point. He must have sat, in his bedroom, maybe, and carefully wound it round. The soft sound that this kind of plastic tape makes as it comes free. The way it softens under even the gentlest warmth from your hands. Somewhere, on the televisions of this same town, they are play-ing tennis. Wimbledon. My sister will be avoiding it, but knowing it's on.

There is my uncle Keith watching television, my aunt Denise coming in and out to ask the score, a player unwinding and retaping the. handle of the racket. The same all the time, when Wimbledon is on. I have been there. I almost am there.

'She doesn't need to do that,' my uncle told me, nodding at the TV, smiling but not looking round at me. 'She's got plenty of rackets ready to go, she doesn't need to retape the handle.'

'Oh Jesus, how do you know this?' said Aunt Denise, she never believed my uncle when he started in on something like this.

'Not for years have players needed to rewrap the handle like that. It's psychology.'

'Maybe it's just more comfortable when she does it herself,' my aunt said.

'Comfort, Denise? They're professional tennis players, they have left comfort behind them! No, she's doing it to get focused. To find her edge. It also messes up the other player, if they are weak in the mind. She's not as good as the other player, but the psychological warfare, she wins every time.'

That was just a weekend ago. Watching tennis and eating bowl after bowl of crisps and peanuts. The angriest one, the leader, is shouting now, but shouting in a whisper, he's furious, I feel his finger pushing into my cheek. It aches, pulls the skin down away from my eye. Some of my spit goes on his finger, I almost apologise.

He's asking me something, but it doesn't make any sense. It's just 'Eh? Fucking what? Eh?'

He must know, he must surely know I have no idea what he's talking about, but he's still demanding a response.

I do not offer a response. I cannot speak. I cannot move. Normally, I am a chatty one.

It's not me, I feel sure they must soon realise. Whoever they think I am, I am not. There has been a mistake. There has been a big, very bad mistake.

The knife is hidden away suddenly. The angriest one sits next to me on the bench, puts himself very close on my right side.

This is the side, I realise, where I had an ear infection last month. The doctor had to suck the pus out of my ear with a huge vacuum. It sounded like wasps, he kept having to stop because I was getting too dizzy. I liked it very much when he rested his arm across my chest. It was tender. He was maybe the same age as my mother. His breath was bitter, but he had soft skin, and perfume. I think of this side as my weakest side.

The boys are piling onto the bench now. Another sits to the left of me. Technically I think of this as my stronger side, I suppose, but that side is also pretty weak. Two others dive onto the bench – they are all in black coats, though it's sunny – smoosh onto the ends and they push in on me, crush me. Makes it look like we're together, like we're friends.

I can smell the angriest one. His coat pumps warm air up into my face as he presses close to me. I wish I couldn't – I feel like he knows I can smell him and this will make it all worse. He will be angry that I can smell on him the unwashed skin, the excessive clothes detergent, the bad breath, adult smells that a child ought not to have.

Someone walks past, a man in his running shorts and sweated grey marl T-shirt. He looks concerned, and then frightened, then just passive. Our eyes meet. The jogger seems for a moment like he understands exactly what is happening here. Like he might try to help me. But then he meets the eyes of the boys next to me.

The man has no power. His age, his strength, his position in the company where he works, his access to credit, all of it is useless. He is right there, but also a million miles away. He looks at the ground. Walks a few more metres before checking his phone is still in his pocket, then he starts jogging. Next, a woman walks past, she's in peach-coloured leggings and a T-shirt made of light material, she looks strong, like she does not take any shit from anyone, I try to meet her eye, but it's the same thing. She gives me and the other boys a suspicious glare. The angriest one glares back. Then, with a tut and shake of the head, she is gone.

I should have said something, but it is too late now. It was already too late when I sat on this bench.

The boys get up and form their circle again. The knife is back. Somehow there is nobody else now. The children playing sound so far away, and yet louder than ever, beating in my head along with the loudness of my blood.

The knife goes into me quickly – once twice three times. There is a fourth and a fifth but I do not feel them I am shocked, cold, I cannot find my breath. The third drive did it; sharp and shallow on my chest at first, then pressed more, there was a punch, a bursting through, and I felt things go very bad. I was divided from the world.

More people walked past, but the boys had me surrounded. Nobody could see what had happened. Even if my sister, even if my mother had walked past at that moment, they wouldn't have seen me. I was alone. Cut away.

The sounds of the playground softened, ended quickly as the sun went down. The boys had long dispersed into the cold. Nobody came for a long time. Then a dog, and the dog's owner. Then a rush of people. Police. My mother.

That night, my uncle came alone, sat on the bench where I was and drank a lot of brandy from a bottle. The brandy bottle had a picture of a sailing boat on it, very beautiful. I could, I found, touch the boat on the bottle, I could feel the soft cloth sails, I could hear the sad songs of the sailors on board, heading nowhere, living a thin life on a white sea. I was afraid to do it, but I realised I could go onto the ship, if I wanted, and slosh about there, looking for whales on the label of my uncle's brandy bottle.

I was drawn back because my uncle was singing. He was singing 'Little Donkey', the Christmas song.

He used to sing to me when I was small and I stayed with him and my aunty. He was shy but he had a good voice. Stronger if he'd had a bit of whisky or something already. But it was a beautiful voice. He sang Christmas songs to me, because he didn't know any real children's songs. And he'd sing drinking songs. The way to go home.

On the bench, with his brandy, he sang jaggedly his encouragement to the little donkey to keep going. Keep going. And I felt ashamed for not being able to keep going as he wanted me to, I felt suddenly very sorry for all of it.

He was very young, my uncle, I realised, as I looked at him without my childish eyes in the way. And inside him, deep in there, his soul was a child. Bolting inside him, dizzy from his drinking. A baby soul really.

Through all of this, I remained seated on the bench. I didn't know where else to go. I felt too ashamed to go home without my body.

My mother came back.

'Why? Why has this happened?' she asked.

'It was a mistake,' I told her. A mistake. Just a mistake.

Her teeth bit the wood of the bench as she cried. I thought it would break her teeth but nothing broke. She left deep marks in the wood, but nobody would ever notice them.

I waited with her until it got dark and she was taken home by her friend, Jacqui. Jacqui was our neighbour. She said, 'Come on darling, let's get you out of this cold. Nothing to do here now.'

'What if he needs me?' my mother asked.

'He's beyond that now. He's not here darling. He's not here. Come.'

My mother followed her without another word. She looked like a stone, a heap of rocks in a barrow being wheeled away.

I watched another night pass. Foxes came along. A cat. One of the boys came, not the angriest one, but another. He stood and looked at the bench. I could hear him breathing. I could see his soul in there, huddled and bothered. Already waiting to be out of this and somewhere better.

My sister has arrived with a paper envelope full of white pages. They are photocopies of a note in my mother's handwriting.

I just want to know what happened to him. If anyone has any infor-mation, I won't ask who you are. I just want to know why this has happened to my son. He was a good boy.

Unlike the boat on my uncle's brandy, I cannot get close to these words, but I stay with them, I linger near them for a time. I feel as though I need to reply, and say I'm OK. I am well, I am sorry.

It's just residue, says the fox when he comes round. You'll soon forget about it and go off. Can't you hear the bell?

Good. I feel relieved that I will soon move on.

The fox has been very supportive. He mentions the bell from time to time. The ringing bell, but he's very supportive, even though this bell does not seem to fit. Very kind, the fox. As have many rats, the souls within them, they speak freely, unlike human souls, which seem dreadfully preoccupied. Although, of course, I have been reassured by the birds, a soul is a soul is a soul, whatever that means.

I know at once that Jacqui would have photocopied the pages using her work photocopier.

The fox is not here right now. As so often seems to happen, I feel alone suddenly, but it usually passes.

I don't know where else to go. I am anchored, it feels like. My ankle is locked into the bench, somehow, through the slats. I can see it, my transparent foot. Don't worry about that, the birds have said. Not a problem, the fox. All of them ignoring the foot anchor problem. A phone is ringing in the lobby. An old-fashioned ring, the phone has an actual bell in it.

The ringing continues for a while and it becomes clear nobody is going to answer. I get out of my leather chair, I lay the newspaper down on the armrest. I leave my coat, but take my case over to the row of public payphones. Each phone has a moulded dome so you have to dip under to pick up. The ringing phone, which I have come to think of as my phone, has a lightbulb pulsing gently. My footsteps echo pleasantly as I approach the phone. My suit is lined with something soft, the trousers hang perfectly, and where they touch my skin (actually a conceptual membrane) I have a barely perceptible sensation of warmth.

My mother, she comes back and back.

I reach the phone, and dip under the domed hood. The light inside is without an obvious source, it forms moving pearlescent colours on the inner surface of the dome. I am holding the receiver to my ear (actually a pleated area of the membrane).

A voice is speaking. A great rain has come, it says. The notes your mother wrote have been soaked and churned up, unread, by the rain. They have crumbled, come apart, been eaten by bugs.

Your mother has decreed that the letters must be laminated.

She is typing them on the computer at home. She is sitting with her back straight on one of the heavy dining chairs that the landlord forced upon us when we moved in. He had nowhere else to store them, he said.

The computer is old. It crouches in the living room. Somewhere inside the large, mostly hollow tower, a dusty fan hisses and generates more heat than it cools away. She spends hours silently begging the printer to work. She will have asked my uncle to get it laminated.

Without moving I can see her. My sister in her ear, offering to type for her. 'It will take me ten minutes, Mum!'

But she does not want it to be ten minutes. She does not allow them to interfere with what she wants to say. She does not let them remove the language.

The laminated messages are pinned to the wood.

They stay for two weeks. Nobody calls except cranks and psychos. My mother talks to them. She listens to them heavy-breathing. She listens to them saying awful things. I deserved it, they say. I was the devil. Sick people who say they don't know anything, but wanted to call and convey how shocked and sorry they were. Some people who had also lost a child called and advised her to take the signs down.

'He's gone. He's not here. He's somewhere else.'

I heard them singing at my funeral. 'Morning Has Broken'. I felt colour return. The song rose around me and I felt bathed in it, warm I felt.

The police tape blows loose. A jogger gets tangled, disgusted, tugs free. They come – the ones who did it. Together then each alone. I see something dark in the water when they are here. They stand and watch the grasses move. They stand for hours in silence.

We have forwarded you a ticket, the voice says. I look in my hand and I am holding the ticket. You will learn a lot on the journey, we hope.

I leave the hotel after waving to the concierge. It feels good to wave. I realise I am breathing again. The streets feel solid, hard lines, browns mustards reds, people walk in peaceful rhythms. The station is not far.

The Durhams

I am in the Durhams' house now – it wasn't hard to find the place, even without my phone. It is a fashionable terraced house, not unlike the one I live in. Bigger, obviously. Much bigger, and in a grander architectural tradition. It has a front door the width of two front doors. Durham is older than me, he bought his house years before I bought mine, so he got a bigger one in a better area. I'm jealous of Durham's house. His walls have so much more surface than the walls in my house, there is more wall everywhere you look, and more floor. The furniture is enormous.

There are pictures around the place; family photographs blown up and mounted in specialist frames. Durham himself is in most of them, glaring out from under his grizzly brown fringe. His family gathered around. I examine each picture in turn, wondering about this man and his family. What were they like, the people who brought him into this world and share it with him? I have never heard Durham's mother's voice, for example. I will never hear it – she is dead. I look at her and try to imagine how she talked. Did she have an accent? What did Durham hear when she praised him, or chastised and mocked him, or consoled him when he was a boy? I cannot know.

I look at the pictures of his wife and son and try to imagine how they feel about being so closely associated with Durham. Do they like him? They seem very happy. They must love him. I am glad. I am pleased to see Durham hasn't passed his ill-tempered face down to his kid. The boy seems unburdened in this picture here, even by the light of my torch, which tends to flash off the glass in the frame. I didn't want to come here in the dark. I actually had no intention of coming here at all. I have been resisting the urge for weeks. But then, in the middle of the night, I decided I had to.

I'm pleased to report that it doesn't stink here or anything. The Durhams took the bins out before they went away, they cleared most of the surfaces, but they left the fridge full of stuff. I'm looking in there now. Nothing unusual going on. Everything looks well preserved. I am actually impressed by the situation in the Durham fridge. Who keeps their fridge in such perfect order? I wonder. Is this a sign of their collective malfunctioning? Is this what called you here, if you have come here?

Running my torch over the kitchen peninsula, I see envelopes with names on. I see clean, dry piles of plates. A chopping board coloured pleasantly with years' worth of beetroot and mushroom dirt. It is wholesome rather than dirty. There are fruit flies on an orange half, the only thing out of place. They shift in the torchlight like iron filings taunted by a magnet.

Looking closer at the family pictures, Durham's son, who is older than my son, looks sweet, if somewhat obedient. He's smiling in a school uniform here. In this one, the uniform of the Cub Scouts. I feel bad about the boy. I don't want anything to happen to him. I hate to think he might actually be scarred by all this. I don't want anything to happen to any of the Durhams, not really. I'm climbing their stairs. The light from my torch shrinks as I climb into the darkness. The light becomes thin. I shine it around but instead of showing me banisters and the expensive runner, there's just light coming back, like sunlight on a river. I keep walking up the stairs. Details clatter away. I can hear the sound of myself breathing. I can hear my voice, this voice, this voice if that's what it is. Doing this. These words and nothing else. As I reach the landing I catch my foot. I'm falling in darkness. My spine shivers, bracing for impact. I try to detect a row of tents, or a flash of grass, something that will hold me still.

I am on the floor, but still falling. I feel my fingers touching surfaces I know to be furniture, but they slip away. Why have you come here, Benjamin? This question is on the air, cold as the leg of the occasional chair that the Durhams keep next to their massive bespoke bookshelf. I feel like screaming. I feel convinced that I am no longer alone. I continue to fall, and yet I remain on the landing of this tasteful, well-proportioned house. I am in the Durhams' house and I cannot leave.

Durham used to eat lunch with people, that was his thing. Anytime I was in the kitchen area, there would be Durham entertaining like we were not in a professional communal space, but a venue he had hired. Kebabs with the sales team. Health bowls with the developers. He was into the street food market near Old Street, and he would go with his chosen group every day. I never ate lunch with Durham. I could have done if I wanted, he was not exclusionary, but I liked a sandwich and crisps. One time he was eating a soup and making everyone smell it. He beckoned to me, 'Come and smell this soup!'

I smiled, kind of thrilled by the prospect of how disgusting the soup was bound to smell. Then I realised he had not been beckoning me, but someone behind me — a woman I didn't know at all. I was forced to swerve away, down the staircase to the tenth floor where I remained hungry and unsatisfied for the rest of the day. Durham didn't notice, of course. He probably never meant to insult me.

Durham was his last name, but he never used anything else. Even his email signature, which I felt sure was autogenerated, just said Durham.

'People call me Durham,' I heard him say once to a swoggle of interns at a Thursday mixer. He said it like the severance of his first name (Dean) had been out of his hands. This bothered me. What was behind this need to be associated with the word Durham, and which Durham did he mean? The city? The county? The university maybe. I didn't know which. All of them I suppose.

I left that company months ago, and I forgot about Durham and his lunches and his last name. But then I saw him one bright morning in the lobby at my current place.

'Wow, Dean!' I said. He was standing by the lifts with a dumb smile on his face.

'It's still just Durham.'

I nodded at this, apologised with a laugh. We stood quietly for a moment, neither of us with anything worth saying. I couldn't even raise the energy to ask about his family. I felt more and more relaxed as I realised he was nervous about working here (though not *here*-here, because now, as these words come to me, I am in Durham's house), in a place this enormous. His age seemed to rest heavier on him in this vast building. I was glad. I was glad too that in a place like this nobody could ever smell anyone else's soup. There were too many other soups that would get in the way. A society exists here that he could never hope to dominate.

I was thinking about his lunch obsession, and of all the many hundreds of chairs and tables in this office's canteen, and how I would basically never have to see him eating ever again if I didn't want to, when I said, 'We should catch up soon.'

He agreed, but we never set a date. I didn't think of Durham very much. I saw him from time to time. He gave muted waves. Nods of the head. We kept a respectful distance from each other; we had come to an understanding.

I say all this (am I saying it? What actually is this that I am doing?) to demonstrate how little Durham meant to me. Nothing at all. Less, certainly, than the city or the county or the university – none of which I have ever visited.

He vanished from my life, until one Thursday, when I saw him among a posse of lunch-people heading out through the lobby into the plaza. There he goes, I thought. He was near the back of the crowd, trying to keep up. He didn't even notice I was there as he passed by. I was thin air to him all over again. I felt a sense of relief wash through me and went back to my lush, pressure-free sandwiches and my unimportant, boring work.

About a month after this sighting, I got the first email.

Subject: Sister
Hi Ben, I need to talk to you urgently about a
personal matter. It's about your sister. My wife
and I want to meet with you outside work.
Soonish if poss. Durham

I didn't bother replying. I actually had a deadline for once, and I assumed Durham was trying to be funny. Or that possibly he was feeling lonely and was scrabbling for friendship – possibly after embarrassing himself at some post-work event. It felt like a stretch, but then the people here would not appreciate his smelly soup antics, I was sure. It felt like a vapid overfamiliarity that had no real weight. Maybe there was someone else the email was meant for. Ben Peston. Len Rester. Could've been either of those people, they both existed on the internal directory.

But a small part of me wondered. What if it was meant for me? What then? What did he want? The man knew I had a sister. It was one of the only things he knew about me – that my sister was an academic. He knew this because she had come to the old office once, having just returned from a conference in Durham. We were going to see our brother, Tom, and take him out on the town.

'This is my sister,' I'd told Durham. 'She's been in Durham.'

'I'm sure I would have noticed!' he'd said.

Even though we ignored this terrible joke, Durham insisted on leaving the office with us, walking us to the station. All the way he asked imbecilic questions about what the point of academia was, to the extent I had to apologise for his behaviour. We had to explain it all to Tom, who, of course, found it hilarious.

Maybe Durham's been drinking at lunchtime, I thought. Though it was still odd that he mentioned his wife.

I continued not to reply. I continued to be distracted.

Maybe my sister's said something controversial about wives, I thought. Maybe it triggered him. This was very possible – in the *Guardian* maybe. Or maybe she visited the University of Durham again and he was reprising his old joke. Or she'd ridiculed the city/university/county of Durham in some way, and he expected me to grasp the connection.

In any case, I put his email in the low-priority folder and pressed on with my work. Durham followed up a day later. This time by direct message.

Hey mate! Really need to grab you for a sec, but can't get into the office atm. I'm remote working. Can you meet me?

Sorry Durham. I am super busy at the moment. TBH I never really speak to my sister. Not sure how I can help.

FFS

Eh? Listen, I am really busy atm. Please just email me or whatever, but if it's anything about my family, I would prefer you to leave it alone. This is really not cool actually. I'd like it to end.

Was I shaken? Yes. But I remained outwardly calm. I put 'do not disturb' on the chat and took screenshots. I created a folder called 'Durham HR'.

I went back to my feebly progressing work. I thought about sending a text to Mum or Tom to see if they knew anything about the Durhams, but I didn't want to have to explain the whole thing so I left it.

Then another email came.

Subject: Invitation / check on your family
Hi there, this is Samantha, Durham's wife. He is
typing this as I speak to him. I want you to know
this because I want you to picture me standing here
talking to you. Asking you as directly as I
can to take this seriously.

I am urging you to please come and see us.
Normally I would invite you to our home, but I
can't. We are staying in a hotel outside of the city.
We can't enter our house. Your sister is there.
She won't leave. I'm at my wits' end. She appears
on the stairs. She howls and she makes noises
like a crow and other beasts. I need you to help
us. I think your sister has died and that she is
haunting us.

The message went on to imply that the Durhams had not budgeted for any hotel stays. It was something they were unable to afford to continue doing, nights on end, at over £70 per room.

We're having to go down the corridor to see our boy.
He's all alone at night. God knows what he can hear
through the walls in this place.

I replied immediately, regretting being sucked into this non-sense even as I typed.

> Maybe this is a joke. Maybe you've been hacked.
> Either way, since you have brought money into
> it, and children, I'll answer frankly. It's obviously
> impossible what you're saying. As far as I'm aware
> you've never met my sister. I'm not even prepared
> to concede to you that I have a sister. Durham (your
> husband) and I used to work at the same company
> and that's about the only contact you have ever had
> with my family, or I with yours.
>
> I'm clearly not going to agree to pay for your hotel
> bill. I have no suggestions for the collective psychosis
> you appear to be experiencing. You have my
> sympathy. I can recommend family counselling –
> this is not intended as an insult, I myself have been
> through family counselling, and couples therapy, and
> hypnosis. All of these things have beneficial qualities
> for social groups experiencing unusually high levels
> of stress. Or maybe you should take the money
> you're wasting on a hotel in the suburbs and go on an
> actual holiday.
>
> If this was indeed a joke and I've somehow missed
> the point, I apologise. Work has been manic
> recently, and I'm not on my best form.
>
> Either way, my best wishes to you all.
> Ben

I was annoyed that I had replied, especially in a way that went along with the stupid things Durham was saying. It seemed clear to me that he had written that message, and his wife had no idea that he was using her name. He was having a breakdown. I wondered if I should talk to one of the mental health first-aiders about it, but I thought that my reply might implicate me, that I might have made things worse. I felt sure there was some training I'd taken, a quiz that had asked what I should do when faced with a crisis of this kind. I probably knew at the time of the training that the correct answer was not to berate the colleague in distress. I definitely would not have said that the best course of action was to play along with the delusion. As the afternoon wore on, and nothing came into my inbox – from the Durhams or from HR – I let the issue go and switched my attention back to the deadlines.

Only my denial of having seen my sister nagged at me. I had seen her. I had seen you. Only a couple of weeks ago you were in town for an hour, and we ate breakfast at a cafe near the station. We gave your dog a bowl of water.

'It's all she wants these days,' you told me.

'I feel the same way,' I said.

Your dog and I drank a lot of water that day, and I kept texting you later to say that I was in various different places asking to use the bathroom. I'm in the Guildhall School of Drama and I am asking to use the bathroom. I am in the London Transport Museum and I am asking directions to the facilities. I am in the Royal Academy with a high-end cake, hoping to go to the toilet soon.

I laughed quietly each time, as though you were there with me. Which of course you were, really. You were in the space we make for each other. I am aware that you are summoned by these messages I send you. It has been the same since we were children. We have this space and we have permission to summon each other into it. Sibspace. Though I've only started to call it Sibspace now, in later life. And only in my mind – I would hesitate to use that word out loud. It ruins it a bit. But that's what it is. I can send a message or phone you up and your voice, you, enters Sibspace and we give each other our time. Sibspace is so embarrassing. I can sense you wincing at it. What does it mean, Benjamin? It doesn't matter. We are close.

I felt ashamed for telling Durham we don't see one another any more. Alone in my kitchen in the dark I imagined you going to the Durhams' instead of coming to me. I wondered if you had tried to visit me in Sibspace and somehow ended up at the Durhams' house instead.

I tapped a message to you on my phone: Are you haunting the Durhams? Are you alive? I deleted it. I was too afraid of what the answer might be.

I tried calling your number but my phone made a strange robotic noise, which I remembered it making on past occasions when I tried to call you and it turned out your phone was in a canal, or you had smashed it by accidentally dropping it down some stairs.

Alone in the kitchen, alone in my house, I wrote and deleted messages. Would you even receive them? I could not send them anyway. I was afraid of you not replying, or of someone else replying and telling me they were standing next to you, by the side of the road. 'She's not breathing,' they might reply. 'She's not moving at all.'

I watched a video instead, a recent talk you had given.

I watched you there, my sister, moving your arms behind the lectern. After about five minutes – only the introduction – I was completely lost. Your voice was a reassuring burr and crackle, giving knowledge to an unseen audience. Not entirely unseen, there were some heads. Hair and baldness. (All that scalp and hair covering those minds, and all of them listening to you. My god, I still reel from it.) I imagined my own head, seen from behind, a sort of hesitant tonsure. I nodded along to what you were saying. I felt an urgent need to stand up in the audience and say something absurd, or knock someone's hat off. I felt myself reaching out for a man in a hat. But the only hat would have been in a corridor somewhere, I guessed. Or in an office on a hook. I could feel a hook with a hat on it. A very precise form of communication: a hook with a hat on it. I watched you until the end of the video.

Then I called all the hospitals in London, one after another, asking if you or someone fitting your description had been brought in unconscious or comatose. I listened to the space while they went to check, while they looked at records and asked about bodies that had been rushed in through the emergency doors. Are any of these women comatose? Are any of them haunting a finance guy and his family? I had to wish then that they were all other people's sisters. I had to wish someone else was in there and they were not you. I told the people who answered the phone that I prayed there was nobody else there at all. Empty hospitals, I said. I hope for row after row of unoccupied beds. They could hear that I was emotional, but they were busy, so the conversations were rarely satisfactory. Yes, lots of people hurt, and no, none of them are your sister. I called back each of them – can you go and check again – I sat in silence.

I crept towards the space I found in front of me, there in the silence. I pressed ahead while I waited for the hospital to check for your body. To see if it was there. I pressed towards a beige area, and there was a sound like the tearing open of a cracker box.

The fragrance also was of crackers – soft dust, grain, pressure, air. When we did not like the school dinners, these were the crackers they gave us, caked in white spread and liquid jam.

After some sensory adjustment, it felt natural to arrive at the reception area for a medium-sized campsite. It was a lodge, in fact. A reception lodge for a campsite. There was a desk with blocks of paper for guests to make notes. I touched some of the notes and the voice of the woman on the phone, the woman at the hospital, told me there was nothing and nobody matching the description

I had given. I turned over the pages and the voice was gone. Had I said goodbye?

Durham started coming back to the office after a few days' absence. He would make excuses to come to my floor and hang around near the artworks. He'd not been looking after himself properly. He stank of mildew – of clothes taking too long to dry. His trousers were ruckled with creases. He clearly still considered me responsible for the situation he was in. I avoided his eye in every circumstance, even in the meetings he now seemed to attend, even though we worked on different projects. Nobody challenged his presence in these meetings. He just turned up. I couldn't stop him. It would've looked worse for me than him if I'd demanded he leave a meeting on a project, and it turned out he had a key role I didn't know about. I had to put up with him, and his stench.

I left the meetings before they were over, to keep away from him, but then Durham managed to corner me in the bathroom.

'Look what she's done now,' he said, and he demonstrated that his jaw had become massively elasticated. His lower jaw hung open like the cargo bay of a jumbo jet. Inside there his wet tongue dangled about, rubbery.

'Jesus,' I said. 'That's disgusting. See a doctor.'

'It's the ghost of your sister! She's cursed me!'

'This is absurd,' I told him. 'This isn't my sister's doing. Go see a doctor.'

I thought he was going to punch me. He was definitely thinking about it. I informed him that I was keeping a file about him and that I would be showing it to HR.

'How do you know it wasn't your sister?' he asked. 'Have you seen her recently?'

He lifted his jaw back into place before he spoke. It seemed stable but loosely articulated, like a child's swing. The effect was worsened by Durham's tendency to thrust his chin forward each time he challenged me with a question.

'No – my god, I told you, I haven't been in touch with her for years. We keep our lives separate. I think we Zoomed at Christmas. But that was months ago, obviously. This has nothing to do with me. Leave her out of this,' I said.

'She might have died,' he said. 'And you wouldn't know.'

'She hasn't died,' I said, but my voice wavered. 'If she had died, I would have been informed.'

'She might have been in an accident.'

'No.'

'But you haven't seen her.'

'I would have been told!' It annoyed me that I was raising my voice. What if someone heard us? I took a deep breath. Before Durham could start up again, we were interrupted by Simon, one of the developers I work with. He looked at us awkwardly as he went for a cubicle. I took the chance to leave the bathroom and escape to my desk.

I wrote and deleted several more texts to you. I wrote and deleted several more texts to Mum, and to Tom, our brother. What would he do in this situation? Something good and honest, and let's face it, with Tom this just wouldn't be happening. Durham would've just taken him for burgers and been happy. Everyone would have been happy.

I looked up your name on the internet to see if you had died. I tried to talk to you in my mind.

I saw Durham again later, at another meeting, his sad jaw swinging. Also, the skin under his eyes was drooping away from his eyeballs like warm putty. Was this supposed to be my fault too? My family's? He kept smoothing the skin back into place and blinking rapidly. His ears were showing signs of running, an odd liquid like syrup trickling down his neck.

He left the meeting early, no longer interested, giving one-word answers to complex technical product questions. He was broken. I stayed at the office as late as I could to avoid thinking of him in that state.

On my way home, I passed a hotel. I did not recognise it, but I felt certain it was the hotel that the Durhams were staying in. I looked at the square lights of the windows for a long time. I listened as the reception doors opened and closed, like the building was breathing.

I called you, but a boy answered.

'Who is this?'

'George Durham,' said the boy. He sounded morose.

I looked at my phone. I was sure I had tapped your name to make the call, but it just said Durham. I had called Durham's phone.

'I'm sorry,' I said. Then I hung up.

I tried calling you again, but this time I was connected to a hospital. I tried again and this time it was my work answering machine. I stayed on the line and listened to the sound of my office, empty and whirring.

In the dark, in the kitchen, it grew late.

The hospitals told me to stop calling. The police told me to stop wasting their time. I wrote and deleted more text messages.

I called what I thought was your number again, and this time I got through to an answering service.

I left a message. I explained that I was worried, and that we hadn't been in touch in a while, and that I had lost my way of contacting you. Something was wrong with my phone, I explained.

I said I wanted to go back to when we were kids, and Sibspace was just your bedroom door. I would knock on the bedroom door, and you'd have to turn off the music, and I would say something to try and make you laugh. And then I'd come in and try to make you laugh. And then I'd go, because inevitably I would just be taking up space, stopping you from doing what you wanted to do.

In the dark, in the kitchen, the beige area presented itself to me.

I moved towards the beige area. I progressed through the sensory alterations of the sweet reception lodge light. On the desk, a cork-ball key ring with a fluorescent ribbon rested near the desktop computer monitor. The key ring had a label that said Shed 1–5. I wondered if you were now represented here by the cork-ball key ring. It wouldn't surprise me. We have been in places like this, hungry for the campsite shop, wondering if we can play table tennis, trying to get things and to possess things.

I moved through Sibspace. There were empty chairs for waiting. The wood-framed glass door was set into a long window that overlooked the campsite.

I took this to mean you were not outside.

Through the window it was possible to see tents and cars, the white bellies of caravan roofs arched in the sun, swingball spikes with fresh tennis balls hanging slack, awaiting the bat.

I took this to mean you were not in the toilets or a cupboard.

I could hear the sound of tent-awning wind chimes ringing softly somewhere. I could hear a portable heater blowing dry heat at ankle height. This was the language of Sibspace, a burr in the throat.

I knew without having to travel anywhere that the reception lodge had toilets and to get to the toilets it would be necessary to pass the games room. In the Sibspace games room, of course, the games were not true games, but representational areas where amusing concepts we consider related to one another could gather and spend time. I became two unmoving table-tennis bats and sought your attention.

Nothing changed. Not even the cloud in the sky which I could see through the games room skylight.

I moved through the air. I heard a voice but it was only our mother, who was a telephone table and chairs. She could not respond to anything I was saying, and I could not respond to anything she was saying. She was agreeing with the radio. She was agreeing that it is really jam-making that completes the scene of a contented allotment life. The dog concurred, I understood. You were not in the games room.

I felt our mother say, Of course she's not in the games room, but that sentence could have been related to anything. *The Archers.* Anything.

I visited the shop and I lay in wait as a multipack of small cereal boxes. I cried a great deal. I cried because you did not respond and I was worried then, as worried as a small box of Rice Krispies could be.

A horrible thought occurred to me. I wondered if Durham had been here. That lunch-boggling man in my reception lodge!

So I went outside the lodge, into the grassed camping areas. I moved slowly, and everything was slow. The air had caught in it the smell of warm car interiors. 'Where are you?' I called, and my voice now took the form of barbecue smoke and confident familial discipline. A telling-off out of sight, an argument about boundaries in the surrounding fields. This was me begging for a sign that you had not died or been harmed or slipped in the bath.

Our brother Tom found me like this. He put his warm hands on my shoulders. He had been in a tent, he told me. An amazing tent with six individual rooms inside it.

'Holly is haunting the Durhams,' I said, and he laughed sweetly at the idea, and said how wonderful this was, to be talking again after what had felt like a long time, and that I should try to be happier and feel lucky, because I was lucky.

'I'm sorry I didn't tell you,' I said, or tried to say out loud. 'I didn't want to make you worried or upset.'

I smiled somehow (I don't know how, some dust may have risen, not all of the required actions made sense beyond a physical sensation). I smiled at all of the things our brother was saying, and Tom sent the wind through the wild grasses in the casually swollen fields in order to reassure me, yet again, that my years of arrogance and bullying when we were children had been forgiven, he felt sure. Probably forgiven.

Night fell and I became cold on the lawn. Shapes that had once been bright motorhome windows became liquid, tents pooled and dissolved into darkness, the hills and grass failed, familiarity eked away and the reception lodge dwindled into nothing.

I am in Durham's house, falling into darkness, and I cannot hear you. I can hear only this voice (what even is this, this, what I'm doing now?). I'm falling still, continuing to fall, and to speak to you here, in the dark. I remember almost nothing. I can hear only this voice, and I think that somewhere you may be dancing, and having a good time.

A goshawk

Following the latest interest rate hike by the Bank of England, many office workers came home to find that their stepfathers had returned, and were living there now. In all cases, they had returned from the dead, this was agreed. Even though many of them – a majority in fact – had not actually existed before. They were new. They were returned from the dead. When you tried to argue this, the feeling for the argument seemed to melt away. Newsreaders were forced through the contradiction of this on a kind of soft energy. It was never part of any debate – it was just a way of coming into the world.

The stepfathers were fungible, it was said. None of them seemed to be as they had been. Even the many stepfathers that had *not* been, they were substantially changed now.

Sol, whose stepfather did not come back, lived alone at this time. Everywhere he looked, the stepfathers were there on the news. There were pictures of them, with five o'clock shadows and deep lines across their foreheads. Lost brown eyes.

He tried not to involve himself in the stepfather discourse. Online, he looked at sporting news, which referenced stepfathers only in passing. They asked stepfathers, for example, to text in with their favourite team. Was it the same team they used to support? How had their views changed in the time before they came back?

Sol swerved these articles.

There was a great deal of speculation regarding the stepfathers. For example, where had they even gone, before returning?

Nobody remembered them going anywhere in order to return. But they were *back* now so they must have gone. Nobody could deny it.

It was a police matter, but very few removals took place. Many international news outlets were intrigued, but none of them could explain where the stepfathers had been all this time. The police said it was going to take time to answer all the questions everyone had. Lines of enquiry dried up quickly because everyone now had an extra mouth to feed, including many hundreds of members of the police force.

The stepfathers were gentle and awkward. They wore slippers. They had a tendency to go from the front of the home to the back of the home to check the weather at both ends. They drank water, orange juice, tea and coffee all from the same mug. They would sit all day wondering what that alarm was, it was definitely coming from the street, but they would not go outside the front door to look.

On the news at nine o'clock, Mike Jones, a husband and father from Fleet in Hampshire, described the arrival of a stepfather in his home.

'Well, of course, he is the kids' stepfather, but I am their real father. My wife and I have only ever been married to each other. So in some ways it doesn't make sense. But we're embracing it all.' He was smiling the whole time he was saying this. His eyes sparkling and his moustache stretching, enjoying the shape of his words.

'We're happy to accommodate him to be honest. He's tidy and doesn't talk when the TV is on. He's always around, so we also get free child care! Win-win! And you know, it makes a change from what's normally on the news. It makes a change from hearing about all the wars and immigrants.'

When interrupted by the reporter and then asked about the habits of the stepfather, the man from Fleet said, 'Oh, well, he's quiet. Somewhat shy. He's all right with the kids, though he doesn't seem to do much with them. He doesn't want to go to the park or anything. And to be honest, we are still very cautious about that sort of thing. You can trust him! Of course you can trust him, but only so far. Only to keep things ticking over while you're out, you know? He'll say the right thing when my daughter brings him one of her pictures that she's done, he'll seem impressed by it, or he'll play chess with her – he teaches her all the openings. You know? All that sort of stuff. Seems to know a lot about submarines and plankton, that sort of stuff. Useful to have around. No trouble.'

The footage showed a child playing on the lap of a stepfather. The stepfather was in a dressing gown, sitting in a wing-backed chair with the newspaper. He glanced at the newspaper, but was also focused on keeping the child from falling off his lap as she played.

Sol turned off the television. The room was silent and dark.

'Turn the lights on, could you?' he called, but there was no response. He was talking to a stepfather who wasn't there. He'd been trying this sort of thing with increasing desperation for a few days now. Maybe his one was just late arriving. Or it had become snagged somehow on something.

'Was that the door?' he'd said on the Saturday morning just gone. 'Could you check, please? I'm in the middle of something.'

Of course, he'd opened the door himself. There was nobody else there to do what he was asking. And of course there was nobody at the door either. It seemed that nothing at all was actually happening in Sol's life. He wondered if it was a curse. He wondered if he had been omitted somehow from some list that everyone else was just on by default.

It was something he felt a lot – a light, spongey feeling in his stomach and his mind ran and ran and ran over the fact that his stepfather had not returned.

Sol had actually *had* a stepfather, unlike millions of people who now had one 'return' to them. This was a slap in the face. He had loved the man very much, though he had been careful of his mother's own feelings when on the phone to her of late. Their brief calls never covered events in the news, and it felt normal to just not mention stepfathers at all. She knew he didn't have one return. He knew – or was 99 per cent sure – that she also had not had one return.

Sol knew there were more like him out there. The stepless, he called them. There was a guy in Essex who appeared on the news regularly to say there should be tax breaks for those who had to cope alone without a stepfather.

Sol had tried the online groups, and even a physical meet-up, but it was no good. The people there didn't seem bothered. Or if they were bothered, they were bothered in the wrong way.

At the last meet-up he went to, a man called Matthew tried to get him to agree to take it in turns to wear a dressing gown and slippers and go round to each other's houses.

'No thanks,' Sol had said. Then he'd said he needed the toilet, and slipped away home. He never contacted those people again.

For Sol, it was easier to think that everyone's stepfather had returned except his own, and he was alone.

Sol's stepfather – his real one – had not been anything like the ones that were coming back. He had been a difficult man, but not shy like these ones seemed to be. He had been a huge personality. In Sol's formative years, the arrival on the scene of this interesting man had probably saved his life. His little town existence had suddenly become full of colour, now that this strange, whisky-drinking outsider had come in and shaken it about. Sol believed this absolutely. Despite the baggage and the difficulty of the adapted morning routines, and the food he suddenly was not allowed to eat because it specifically belonged to someone else. Amongst all of the trials, there had been a radiation of love from this man, whose belongings were regulated, but whose soul was not.

Sol missed him. And he had not come back.

'You OK, old chap?' he might have said if he had come back with the other gown-wearing men. 'I'll put a light on, eh? Don't want your eyes shrivelling up like raisins!'

Sol turned the lamps on himself. He tried to read a book, and after a while he put the television back on. Nothing happened – the people on the television competed with each other to prepare the best food, but Sol was not interested in them. A stepfather had entered MasterChef, but was eliminated in week three. He seemed close to tears in his elimination piece to camera.

'I had such a wonderful time with you all. Just brilliant. Sorry. Ugh, sorry I couldn't do more.'

Sol ate dinner in the kitchenette at the small table. He had potato waffles, sausages, gravy from very old granules. He did not feel like a grown man. Peas also.

About halfway through eating, he felt a chasm of loneliness open up within him. All he could do was cut more waffle, more sausage, scoop it through the gravy to send as bolus into the chasm.

He kept going until it was all gone and the chasm ached at the edges and went numb.

He sent messages to his friends. Sandy and Harry, Jon, John, Jonathan and Jen. The group was called 'The Johns' but it included loads of other people.

'Bored,' he wrote. 'Who wants to save me from sitting alone eating wasabi nuts until I'm dead?' He was not sure why he lied about wasabi nuts. He didn't have this snack in his house. These kinds of lie were coming out of him more and more these days. Since the stepfathers came back. Since the interest rates went up. He lied about snacks, he lied about books he was reading, about films he had seen.

'Soz lad,' came the replies. All different versions of Soz lad. When did people start saying this? Soz lad! Even Sandy, who never usually adopted these catchphrases. Soz lad!

It was, Sol knew, something they were getting from the step-fathers. There were several Soz Lad memes already. A stepfather would be wearing an apron over his dressing gown, holding a spatula or a football or a hammer and looking stern or perplexed. 'Soz lad!' It would say in large white letters. Sol had no idea what it was supposed to mean, but it was everywhere. He guessed that all the stepfathers had this habit of saying 'Soz lad.' When they fucked something up.

It was the kind of thing he felt unable to ask about. You have to know the steppies, came the answer. I don't know how to explain it if you don't know the steppies.

Only one reply was different to the others. From Jen, 'I'll DM you,' she said.

A few seconds later, the direct message from Jen. 'Need a huge favour. I can't ask anyone else! But it will be easy, and it will get you out of the house.'

Sol knew immediately that Jen's request would be either gross or inappropriately demanding, or cost him money. Jen had been asking Sol for favours of this kind for years. He sighed and did the washing-up while he contemplated the idea of doing someone a favour.

Jen's requests were rarely boring – and pretty much anything that got him out of the house felt like not a bad idea.

He looked at his dirty plate. The blank thoughts he was strug-gling with these days glistened in the emulsive remains of cold gravy. He replied to Jen before he had time to think about it any more.

'Sigh. Sure, what is it?'

'Ugh it is quite gross so I'm just going to ask and you can just answer and not be weird about it, OK?'

A sort of sick feeling was beginning to creep into Sol's stomach. 'OK,' he wrote.

'Don't say yes if you're going to be weird about it.'

Sol checked the group messages to see if anyone else had said yes to his request for just a simple drink at a pub, but no, it was all just Soz lad.

He replied to Jen. 'OK, yes! I'm in. Whatever it is, yes. I formally say and attest that I say yes to your weird request.'

'Because being weird would not be OK, yeah? This whole favour is about improving an awkward situation, not making it worse.'

'FFS Jen, what is it?'

'OK, you know me and Tony are trying at the moment? As in TRYING right? Well, since the steppy got here the vibe has been a bit weird.'

'Right . . .' Sol wrote. He was very glad that this conversation was not happening face to face, or even using spoken language. He watched the dots as Jen typed her reply.

'OK OK OK. He's not trying to be creepy or anything, but he's always THERE. He just sits in silence, right? And I have this app. And when my app bleeps, me and Tony have to go to the bedroom, NO MATTER WHAT. But once we get into the room, we can hear Steppy moving around. He comes to the bedroom door. He just stands there. Mood death. No baby. If you ever really meant what you said about being a fun uncle, you're gonna have to get involved in making it happen. Ugh I might not send this. Don't be weird don't be weird don't be weird.'

Sol was breathing heavily, his blood felt gloopy. Why was he so embarrassed? It was fine. He took a breath. Briefly he looked in the mirror in his hall, his cheeks were red-blotched. He wrote: 'Yikes OK. Jen, you know something? I am fine with this. I thought it was going to be like a donor situation? Like you were gonna ask for my seed?'

'Eh? GROSS. NO. You agreed not to be weird.'

'No, I'm not saying I would've said yes to a donor situation. Ugh sorry. OK, I can definitely help. Do you want to use my flat or something?'

A long long time passed before he heard anything back.

'No! Not your flat. No offence but your place is not the vibe. What I need is someone to come over and sort of sit with the steppy while me and Tony get some time to ourselves. Can you do it? If yes please hurry because the app is going to bleep at me any minute now.'

Sol groaned, but it was too late to stop this. It was going to happen.

'Just to be clear,' he wrote, 'you want me to sit with your returned stepfather while you try to get pregnant in your room?'

'Yes.'

'With Tony?'

'Sol! I warned you, didn't I? Yes with Tony. Tony and me are having a baby. I love him. Will you help us or not?'

Sol returned to the kitchen. One last look at the plate on the tiny, sad little table. 'Gross. OK.'

'A FACE WITH HEARTS FOR EYES. Do you want me to order you some food?'

'No, I've eaten thanks.'

He binned the gunk from his plate.

'Kk, don't be long please. Bleep imminent.'

Fucking Tony, Sol thought, but fine. He prepared himself to leave.

The whole area where Sol lived frightened him these days. The garages, the concrete bunker that served as a wholesaler to local off-licences and mini supermarkets, the corner where a gang had cycled past him one day and the leader had slapped him on the top of the head before cycling away.

Below all his other desires and thoughts, there was this need to get out of the area where he lived. People said the stepfathers had brought with them a sweeping reduction in crime. They had made public spaces cleaner. The streets were empty. The air clicked with loneliness. Sol did not feel safe until he was on the bus and heading away from it all.

Jen lived in the middle of a new development. Her block was finished and about half-occupied, but she was surrounded by diggers, cranes and heaps of earth and concrete.

After a few minutes searching, he realised he was lost in the faceless avenues of the building site. The navigation on his phone did not understand where he was, the postcodes were not recognised. He had no choice but to press on through the boarded straights, images of the bodies of men and women shaping down at him, from promotions for the gym, from deep L-shaped sofas, the exciting future inhabitants of the unbuilt flats.

He had an idea that there was a gate he would need to call from.

Up ahead of him, he heard the sound of someone breathing, lightly cursing. Emerging from the boarded alleyway, Sol found himself in a space that was probably once a car park, and was now a not-yet-landscaped communal grounds. In the damp floodlights, there was a man kicking puddle water. It was a stepfather.

'Hey, are you OK?' Sol called out. The stepfather didn't seem to hear him. He just kept skipping into the shallows of this huge puddle and kicking his faux-moccasined foot across the top. The slipper, now soaked, skimming across the surface, sending up an arc of water.

Sol got closer. It was amazing to see a stepfather like this, outside, alone. It seemed to have lost its mind a little bit. The neck was red and fleshy, the line of his grey-white T-shirt was pulled out of shape. The trousers were frayed. Sol took a picture on his phone. He took more, the stepfather didn't seem to notice.

'The thing to look out for is when the algae is a blue-green colour,' the stepfather said, and then 'Ye! Ya!' as he kicked out again over the puddle.

Around the eyes and nose of the stepfather's face, Sol could see the remaining traces of bruising. Yellow patches blossomed across its cheeks, hard black troughs gathered light under the bottom lid of the left eye.

'Hey are you OK? Should I call someone?'

Sol started to dial 999 but didn't actually press the dial button. Should it be 111 first? Or just, what, send a text to the police? He realised he didn't know what to do. He started googling for answers, but then the stepfather started talking again and he stopped.

'Blue-green algae could be harvested and used as a biofuel, it has been widely researched, but the government don't know where to get the water from. But it's an amazing product, ya! Ye ya!'

Sol stepped back to avoid getting splashed by the puddle. Around the stepfather's neck was a troubling red line of bruising. From the pocket of its dressing gown peeped the broken remains of a World's Best Stepdad mug. Sol could almost touch the step-father, he was so close.

He was raising a hand to its shoulder when a cold voice behind him said, 'Leave it mate.'

'Oh!' Sol turned to the source of the voice. It was a young man, maybe nineteen, twenty years old. He was wearing a thin water-proof coat over his hoody.

'I thought he was alone, sorry.'

'Not mine, mate,' the young man said. 'It's a stray.'

Sol noticed that the young man was holding a stick in his hand. It was a pretty casual hold, down at his side, like he wasn't really aware of it, but it was not a casual stick. It was a bat really, it had been varnished.

'I've called an ambulance anyway,' Sol said. 'Should be here soon.'

'Won't come,' said the young man, visibly choosing not to challenge Sol's obvious lie. 'They won't treat them on the NHS. You have to get a vet or something if yours has any issues. Don't you know this stuff?'

Sol kept his eye on the stick in the young man's hand. 'No, I don't really know anything.'

A silence emerged then between the three of them. Sol could not stop looking at the stepfather. His knuckles were purple with cold, and his fingers looked very swollen. As he shuffled back and forth, mouthing facts about blue algae, his dressing-gown sleeves rucked up, revealing more of those burnt-on lines.

'I think someone has been hurting him,' Sol said. 'He needs help.'

'They do this to themselves,' the young man said, waving the bat. 'They lose it and go out into the street. I saw two of them fighting last night. Fucked each other up.'

'Well, the ambulance will be here soon.'

'Course it will.'

Sol was shaking as he stared at the young man who was still just letting that stick hang there. When his phone started vibrating in his pocket, he almost jumped out of his skin. It was Jen.

'Where are you, Sol? Don't tell me you've bottled it.'

'I'm here now, yeah. There's a stepfather looking confused and I think hurt.'

Sol tried his best to make it look like he was talking to the ambulance people. The young man looked around at things, at the ground, then back at Sol, as though he had an audience on him, as though the whole world was waiting to see what he would do.

'Yeah yeah, I am in the car park area of the new building complex. Yep. That's right.'

Meanwhile, Jen was saying, 'OK, I can see you. WTF are you talking about? Who's that with you?'

Sol put his hand over the speaker and spoke directly to the young man. 'They're asking if someone will be with him when they get here. Will you be here?'

The young man looked at him for a moment, then shrugged and walked off.

'It's just me,' Sol said. 'See you soon.'

A few minutes later, he was in Jen's kitchen, looking out at the car park area. The stepfather was still there, kicking water.

'He's been hurt,' Sol said.

'Hmm,' said Jen. 'I think he'll be fine.' She was looking at her phone. 'Tony says hi. He's just finishing a work call.'

'Oh, OK. Hi Tony, from me. Do you really think he's OK? It seemed pretty bad.'

'Sol, how many people do you walk past every day who are in a bad way? On the street or whatever.'

'I know. Ugh. I feel like this is different. I should call someone.'

Jen put her phone away with a snap.

'Ambulances won't come,' she said. 'NHS can't help them.' Then she whispered into his ear, 'My app has beeped. I'm going now.'

'Oh right. OK,' he said.

'You sure this is not weird?'

'No, of course, it's fine. Come on, it's us. When was anything normal?'

'Ha. Thank you. I'm a bit nervous.'

She sounded young to him at that point – sort of frightened of it all and embarrassed. Sol nodded.

'Don't be nervous.'

She kissed him on the cheek. It wasn't that bad. He didn't watch her leave. He kept staring at the stepfather, who was still outside. He heard sounds in the flat around him. He became aware of why he was here, and wondered what the sounds were.

'All right there boy?'

Sol turned. Jen's stepfather was there. He looked like he'd just had a shave. He smelt of sweet citrus cologne.

'I'm about to put the kettle on,' the stepfather said. 'Push you to a cup?'

'Oh, yeah, thanks,' said Sol.

'Unless you want something stronger, son?'

The stepfather's face darkened. He darted across the kitchen, opened a cupboard and fetched an unlabelled brown bottle.

Sol remained at the window. The stepfather outside was no longer visible

'Here, you look like you need this, sunshine.'

Sol found he was being handed a glass of clear alcohol.

'What is it?'

'Bit of home brew, that's all. Try it.'

Sol drank the smallest sip from the glass, and felt it spread across his mouth. He coughed.

'Oh ha – not used to it. Don't worry, try again son, go on, try again.'

Sol loved being called 'son'. He drank a bigger sip this time.

'That's it,' said the stepfather. 'You've got to attack it. That's it.'

Sol allowed his glass to be refilled, and went back to looking out of the window.

'Something out there, is it?'

'Someone's stepfather,' Sol replied. 'Looked like it was having some sort of trouble.'

Sol felt Jen's stepfather at his shoulder, the faint brushing of his towelling dressing gown. That citrus smell and the sound of his hand burring against his evening stubble, which was already grow-ing back thick and dark.

After a few moments, he was surprised to feel the stepfather's hand on his back. 'Can't see anything myself. You can't worry about this stuff too much, Sol. Come on mate, come and have a sit down.'

He followed the stepfather to the table, watched him drink some of the clear liquid.

'So, tell me young man, how are things? Work all right?'

'It's OK, I suppose. To be honest, I don't really feel like I'm doing so well lately.'

The stepfather screwed up his face and shook his head.

'What's happening? You been calling in sick? That's all right. You've got to call in sick from time to time. It's good for you!'

'No. I've been going in.'

'Working hard. That's good.'

Sol didn't say anything. He couldn't stop staring at the step-father. He felt strangely at liberty to observe the skin, the reddened areas, the age that was of course no age at all because this step-father had returned and yet never previously existed. He got close enough to smell the breath, which was sharp with coffee and on top of it the powerful drink. Somewhere else there was a tang of bone too, and the slightly sickly smell of babies. A couple of times during this examination, Sol caught the stepfather's eye. It didn't seem offended, but gave a curious fraction of a smile and followed Sol's gaze back to its own chest or the backs of its knuckles.

The stepfather just carried on talking. 'You go in, don't you? Turn up for the people on your team? That's not nothing. You should be proud of yourself. You're doing your best, I can tell.'

'Well …'

'Well what? Hey, look at me. Not there, up here sunshine. Listen, it's clear to me that you take your responsibilities seriously, you go into that office and you greet the people you work with, I can tell. You put your hand in their hand so to speak – maybe not literally, you're not literally shaking hands all day, of course, but you make people feel like they've been seen. They've been noticed, that's you, isn't it? It is – that's you. Invaluable that is. I think you even did it for me when you came in here. You said, "Hello, how are you?" Put me completely at my ease, you did. This is meant to be where I live, but it's you who said hello. Offered me a cup of tea, didn't you?'

'Well, no,' Sol began, but it was no use, the stepfather just rolled over him. Sol drank more of the clear liquid and helped himself to another glass.

'I feel sure you did. This one here is a good one, Jen,' said the stepfather, into the darkness.

'I think she's in the bedroom,' Sol said, quietly.

The stepfather didn't acknowledge this fact. He looked back into the darkness over one shoulder, and then over the other. Beyond the kitchen was the living room and no lights had been left on.

'Jen!' the stepfather called out.

Sol leapt to his feet and strode into the living room. He found the TV remote in the gloom and pressed the standby button.

'Jen!' the stepfather's voice was becoming more anxious. He kept looking over each shoulder.

'I think she's asleep. Do you want to watch a bit of TV?' Sol asked.

'Hmm. I should check on her. Make sure she's settled.'

'I think she's fine,' Sol said. 'Hey look, it's *Springwatch*!'

'Well, no, it'd be *Autumnwatch* now, wouldn't it?'

'Ah, well, anyway – it looks good. *Do* you want a cup of tea?'

'No, sunshine. You sit down, I'll make the tea. I've got Hobnobs too. Don't tell anyone!'

It was *Autumnwatch*, of course, not *Springwatch*. It was, in fact, Sol realised, the late-night/early-morning signed repeat of *Autumn-watch* with the British Sign Language translator in the corner of the screen. There were also subtitles, adding flavour to the footage of the foxes in the golden woodlands.

Sol could feel the stepfather breathing next to him on the sofa. He had made tea, and was resting the cup of tea in the dip of his pigeon chest. Sol swallowed some of his own tea. It tasted strange, the way all tea seemed to taste to him when he had not made it for himself.

'Do you mind if I ask you something?'

'Of course! What is it, Sol?'

'Where were you? Before you came back. What was it like?'

The stepfather sat for a long minute watching a goshawk, and the word 'goshawk' being said by Chris, the presenter of *Autumn-watch*, and the word 'goshawk' being spelled out on the screen in the subtitles, and the actions required to sign the word goshawk.

'Can I ask you a question first?' the stepfather said after the piece about the goshawks was finished.

'Of course.' Sol felt ashamed. It occurred to him that probably you weren't meant to ask stepfathers these questions. It was like the NHS thing, like, everyone knew about it so nobody bothered telling anyone else. Maybe asking them where they came from was what caused them to go mad and go out kicking puddles of water.

'Where were you? Before you were here?'

'You mean before I was born?'

'Exactly, before you were born, where were you?'

'I mean, I don't know,' said Sol, and he wanted to stop talking, but somehow he could not stop talking. He wondered for a moment how strong the clear liquid was that he'd been drinking. He kept going. 'I – I used to think there was a place where you are before you're alive.'

'A place you are before you're alive?'

'Well, yes, a land. I used to say that I could go back there. I used to tell my father about it. He liked hearing about what I saw there.'

'About the land you went to?'

'Yes. I remember the first time I told him about it, he looked at me in the most amazing way. I can remember his smile – I told him I could go there whenever I liked. He just looked at me. Normally, he would have to be off somewhere, he'd say goodnight and then be out of the room and away. But if I told him I'd been to that place, and I'd seen people, then he would stay and listen.'

'A land. I like that.'

'The thing was that when I tried to tell him about it, I couldn't find the words for anything. So I ended up inventing things. It had been real to me, but when I talked about it after, I was just making stuff up.'

Jen's stepfather looked lost in thought at this. His Adam's apple went up and down in a secret little panic, though the stepfather was completely still and seemed fine.

'You still here?' Jen was suddenly in the room.

Sol turned and looked up at her from the sofa. Why did he now feel like an intruder?

'Ah yeah – we were watching *Autumnwatch*. I didn't know how long you'd need.'

'Ha. Not this fucking long.'

'No, I guess. Uh, I should go.'

Sol put his cup of tea down. The stepfather was still sitting silently, looking at the TV as Sol got his shoes back on and prepared to leave.

'Did you and Steppy have a nice time then?'

'Yeah,' said Sol. 'It was actually really lovely.'

'It's good, isn't it? It should be so weird, but it's totally not!'

'No, it's not weird at all. Nothing is. Goodnight Jen.'

'Goodnight Sol.'

Sol turned to say goodnight to the stepfather, but he was now hugging Jen on the sofa.

'Look, Jen, a goshawk!'

Sol let himself out.

Outside, by the puddle, he saw the stepfather from before. It looked even more beaten up now, after the evening with Jen's one, which had been so vigorously clean and healthy.

'Hey,' Sol called to it. 'Hey, it's freezing! You can't stay out here.'

The stepfather continued prattling and kicking water from the puddle. The water had soaked all the way up its pyjama legs now. '... Hundreds of ways that you can help preserve wildlife in your area. It's so easy. Even an idiot like me can do it you just ya ya! Yeee ya! Some goosemeal left out overnight will feed a family of hedgehogs nicely give them a place to sleep but you'll get rats if you don't clean it away in the morning you can't do this in London because otherwise you will be overrun with rats, rats could replace communication systems within the next two years thanks to ye! Ya! Ya!'

Sol stepped closer to the puddle.

'Hey, why don't you come home with me? You look like you haven't eaten. Tomorrow we can sort out getting you back home.'

The stepfather seemed aware of Sol for the first time, and stopped kicking the water. Sol reached out and hooked him by the arm. The stepfather allowed himself to be walked a few metres from the puddle.

Sol found the act of holding him under the arm almost dizzying, the solidness of it, the uncontoured tubular shape of the arm under the dressing gown. And yet weak, so weak, and not quite the expected weight. Lighter, much lighter. Sol felt that he now had complete power over the stepfather.

But when they got to the alleyway, the stepfather found that strength again, an unexpected power, that seemed not to come from musculature or a skeletal frame. The power moved the stepfather's body in the way a plasticine figure might have power if it became animated, the matter itself moving where it wanted to be, rather than because the skeleton was moving.

The stepfather pulled his arm away from Sol, eased him back, turned around and began lecturing the images of people in the photographs on the building company billboards.

'All of these buildings are built too quickly, far too quickly, it will lead to leaks. Not solid. Not fit even for microsubmersion.'

On the word 'microsubmersion', the stepfather lashed out once more with his legs, giving the surface of a small puddle a few skim-kicks, spraying water in a dirty arc.

'Ye! Haho! There are people out there now who still think of underwater habitation as a serious survival option for humans. Aha! I am so sorry to say it, but Atlantis *can't* happen. As painful as it is, we have to let go of our nostalgia for non-evolutionary submersible living – it's not actionable! What would we even ya!'

Sol felt a wave of tiredness come over him; a greying energy and a hunger as he went round the other side of the stepfather and started pushing him, shoving him along the alleyway.

'It's not safe. You need to get indoors,' he said. He kept saying things like this, like 'please', even as the stepfather pushed back and made stubborn leaps to the left and right to minimise and evade.

The stepfather grumbled the way a dog will growl from almost silence, rising in menace as you get closer.

'Mmm no!' it snapped suddenly.

Sol flinched but was untroubled, he pulled at the dressing gown, threw the stepfather against the wall.

'You're hurt,' he said. 'You need help.'

The stepfather tried to wave Sol's hands away, they were grappling now. The stepfather's words were thin, general, 'I'll be fine. Leave off! Oh it's nothing, nothing, come on now,' even as he slapped Sol's hands away and pushed him back.

'I have to take a look,' Sol hissed, panting. 'You look badly hurt!'

Sol approached again with his hands raised, and the utterances of the stepfather expanded into flinches and barks, 'Give over! Leave it out! By god!', old-fashioned things, as the stepfather flinched at Sol's touch, but it was weak, in the end. No real power to it.

The stepfather let itself be put in the taxi. Sol bundled it into the back seat where it hissed and shook its head, it looked panicked but weakened. A captive.

Sol pulled the door closed beside him. He felt exhausted.

The driver made a sympathetic face in the mirror.

'They're more trouble than they're worth,' he said. 'There should be a place you can take them – NHS can't take 'em. Doctors say they're not even real.'

Sol looked confused.

'I mean not human biology. Nobody can help you if they go crazy or break a leg. Mine broke its wrist and it was howling. It was awful, we had to put a rag in its mouth. I said to my girlfriend, we didn't ask for this! Still though, free childcare!'

Sol nodded. He didn't say anything.

He was clasping the hands of the stepfather together at the wrist, gripping tight enough to break the skin. And his foot was pressing down, crushing through the heel into the top of the metatarsals of the stepfather's foot, and the way the air was going into him as he breathed did not feel right, and he wondered if his head would stop spinning enough to get up the stairs and get his new stepfather inside.

'The government has a failure of confidence that's why they're turning to ideas like hydrogen, it's a nice dream but what about the cost of infrastructure? If they think the increased water yield required can be taken out of rising sea levels then they're out of their ye yah.'

Celia in the mist

There is a time, just before the sun sets on the village, when the mist that surrounds the dwellings in my area lifts rapidly and then falls back down, as though dragged in by a lung. The light at this moment changes from grey to plum and back again.

My friends often come round to visit at this time. They sit with me; we drink tea at the outside table and wait for the loop in the mist – the small bank that rises and swirls back beyond the field. Each of us has our preferred seat around my table. Or rather, the table outside my dwelling. I do not technically own the table.

My preferred seat allows me to recline just a little bit, leaving my head just a fraction lower than the heads of my guests. It has become my habit to settle back and let the events run over and across me. I relinquish the trappings of playing the host, just for a few minutes. I have a good view of the mist, even through half-closed eyes.

In between them talking, I feel as though the whole place, the village, the surrounding land, the far-off mist bank, is drawing in a breath. I can hear ants slowing down, the beetles.

I listen to my friends telling stories and misremembering things. Celia talks fondly about a brother, Sandy. He used to swim in the river near their home in autumn and winter when it would swell and shimmer under the cold sunlight. He had auburn hair, Celia told us, that fell in front of his face like dead stalks of grass, and he would squint at you and hold his hand up in a little salute. His eyes were tiny grey buttons that seemed to have almost no pupils at all because Sandy was always facing the light. Celia says she remembers the water on his back as he cut against the river's current. His breath that made no sound.

We know not to ask Celia the name of this river, or the town where she lived, or what Sandy grew up to become – because it is very likely that none of these things were real. She had never thought of a boy called Sandy until she arrived at the village. In the village, in her days of learning and activity, Sandy became real to her. A brother to think of. A river to shield her eyes from. We cannot tell her that in reality there is no left-behind Sandy, there is no muscular winter river.

As Celia talks, I like to hold on to her arm and rest my cheek on her shoulder. She is strong under her big jumper, and the way she moves is like the water flowing in her imagined river. She talks again and again about his amazing prowess in the water. His questioning looks. His playfully infuriating manner with their parents. Sandy was always just the other end of the garden, so you had to shout to him if you wanted to tell him something. Or he was just leaving the table as she began to eat. Just closing the front door on his way out into the wilderness. Her brother Sandy is everywhere she has not prepared herself to be. I do not tell her, as I rest on her arm, that I dream of her brother too. Sandy has become one of my most touchable dreams, he carries precious stones in a leather bag.

The mist rises and coils way out at the boundary, and the fragrance of a city murmurs to us, giving us the flavour of our old excitements and dangers. We drink more tea and argue gently about what colour the buses were, and about the possibility of rain like before, and the possibility of more hot water in the pot.

Sail Away Land

You were lying when you said you were busy this evening. In fact, here you are in front of this television. You have not done anything all day. You had that moment earlier with the beetle on your neck, and that's the highest your heart rate has managed to get.

You are watching this. This television. Yes it's me; this is me, I am your television. Remember when you got this television? Yes, with your partner, and how long have we stared at each other since that relationship ended and they packed you in and went off to Sail Away Land? A long time. It's been a long time, and you lied about being busy and now you're watching this.

Shoeberg it's called. Detective Shoeberg. You're about to watch it. You have heard people at work talking about it, and you have found an episode though something went wrong with the recording, and you've missed the beginning. It seems to be about five minutes in. You're about to watch it. But you are not yet watching it. We're sitting here with the information about the programme on the screen. In silence we are sitting here.

Tra-la-la – that's what your partner said, as the car doors slammed – I'm off to Sail Away Land, and then you were alone. You didn't have anyone to talk to.

Tra-la-la. You probably don't want to discuss it.

That was fucked up, wasn't it? When that beetle was on your neck. And normally it's moths you have to stress about. There are so many moths. You have basically already decided that you're going to move house and burn everything you own that's a fabric

– this is the only way you can imagine being rid of the moths. But you're worried about dust. There is so much dust. Dust travels well. And it can harbour moth eggs.

Remember your partner? You bought this television together when it was already basically over. It was bigger really than you wanted. It seemed so ugly and so out of proportion. It seemed like a lake you were expected to house vertically. But over time you got used to the size. Other people's TVs became huge. Your mother for example – oh god.

Enormous TV, your mother. Tiny house. But you know, that's hire purchase. A huge TV is all you can get. If you're poor enough, you'll never be able to afford a sensible-sized TV in your life. You will have to pay monthly instalments for something that will send you insane, it's so enormous. You should help her more. Your mother. Step in. Call her at least.

You should talk to people more. If you talk to people, then you don't leave as many gaps. You haven't spoken to anyone really – not at work and definitely not outside of work – for months. And now, to fill the void left by your silent voice, they have started talking *about* you. They talk about you at work, a lot.

They are saying – and you are pretty sure of this – they are saying that you are shrinking. You have seen chat sidebars, reflected in the glass of the meeting room. They barely try to hide it.

'. . . I know literally shrinking!' Raffa was telling Heidi.

'It's horrible – like – sad to look at. Sad to look at the down-sizer,' Heidi said.

'LOL TF at Downsizer!'

They might be calling you that – Downsizer. You're sure they are in fact, they are all calling you the downsizer. You're so small. Is that why you like this *Shoeberg*? Shoeberg, who is so poor that she can never eat. The detective with no money.

According to the summary, something happened with her pay-roll details when she joined this new police force, and HR are unable to do anything about it. This week Shoeberg has absolutely nothing to eat and she is investigating the disappearance of a cadet.

You are about to watch this *Shoeberg* against my will. I don't think it's what you need.

You're not looking yet. Maybe you won't bother watching. You're looking at your phone. You are researching how to counteract the effects of adult shrinking. Nothing seems to be available. That's a worry.

Return to full size will be difficult, this is all you have been able to glean. Astronauts and racing drivers report losing or gaining height over time, and it can never come back without expensive treatment. You should speak to a doctor. You are sure that you are shrinking much more than an astronaut would.

There is something else as well, something else you have forgotten. Something urgent.

But you're pressing play, of course you are. Remember that beetle on your neck? Ha, oh god. And you cried afterwards, when the panic was just receding, and you were sure you had killed the beetle, you took a breath and that's when everything else just rushed in and you began to cry.

And around the edge of that crying was a sort of glaze, the glaze of the fact that you know in your heart that your clothes dangle from you now, not just from weight loss, but from height loss and general loss of yourself. You are so lost. How will you get back to them, if you can't stop shrinking?

Perhaps the rats could help. If you become small enough. If you become small enough, you could harness one. They can walk a long way, rats. Probably. I'm sure you've watched something on this TV (this one here that is talking to you now. The one that is saying all of this. Whatever this is) about rats. A programme about rats. They can walk a long way, it said. The commentary made them sound so fearsome, these long-range rats. Many thousands of miles, a single rat can walk. Is that right? And although they need water all the time, they can go without sleep for months on end. The details are not exact, but it could be true. A rat, with well-placed sources of water, could walk without needing to stop pretty much forever. Until its feet are finally eroded. Its paws.

I'm begging you not to watch *Shoeberg*. *Shoeberg* will not take your mind off this. *Shoeberg* is not real escapism. The actor who plays Shoeberg has stated publicly that she regrets being involved in the programme. Something was done, she has said, something was done to her performance. Some trick of editing that she never saw in her copy of the script.

In fact, didn't the actor playing Shoeberg die? And the man who played Patrice? I think they are both dead. Within weeks of each other. I am a television, so I could be wrong.

You've pressed play.

Shoeberg is in the office of her superior officer, she has her back to the camera. The walls of her superior's office are dead-body grey, here and there on the walls are pinned-up documents and yellowing notices. The superior officer, whose pale flesh is glancing out through the gaps between the buttons of his shirt, is bawling at Shoeberg. You've seen him before, this actor, he always occupies positions of authority, but always too has shit glasses and clothes that are far too tight. They make his belly poke out, his ties too are always abysmal. He must be sick of the wardrobe departments. How many years has it been, do you think, since this man was given something comfortable to wear on set?

Shoeberg is reacting shakily to her bollocking. We have still so far only seen the back of her head, but she is obviously in trouble for some recent failure or transgression – it's hard to tell because the superior officer's language is general and vague, and you have joined halfway through an episode, in the middle of a series.

What the hell am I supposed to do now? the chief is saying.

It's a real mess! he says.

You've really landed me in it! he says. He rubs his face, done with it all.

You can *still* only see the back of Shoeberg's head, but it's clear she isn't well. There seem to be clumps of hair missing, or at least, the hair is pinned back in an arrangement that speaks of a desperate mind. Her arms look shaky.

You have to wonder, what did this actor put herself through to get into the physical and mental state required for the part? Before you've even seen her face, you remember, was there a story, some time ago, before she died, that the actor playing Shoeberg had to spend extended periods of time in rehab? Wasn't she discovered in a shed at one point? You think it was a shed. Or I think it was a shed. One of us thinks it was a shed — and I am a television.

When she speaks at last, Shoeberg's voice is so shallow, you have to increase the volume. She's whispering an apology — The heating's not working, she says. In my flat, the heating's been off. It's not easy.

Her boss is not impressed.

You get paid, don't you? he says. We still pay you, don't we?

You're not sure of his actual rank. It's bothering you. You never listen to details of this kind. They probably say it all the time, the correct ranks. DCI or something. The programme is probably incredibly well researched. It's you who doesn't know anything — who doesn't pay any attention at all to what's going on around you.

I didn't get my money last month, Shoeberg says. She is coughing. The coughing actually gets in the way of the words of the line.

Boss: What? Well, why didn't you say anything?

Shoeberg: I talked to payroll. I told them [more coughing].

Boss: Well, you must have messed something up, mustn't you? You're always skimping the details, Shoeberg! Now you're complaining to me that your flat is cold. I suppose you haven't eaten either?

Shoeberg coughs for absolutely ages before answering. In another programme, you would think that this is actually someone who has been poisoned, but the superior officer is not reacting as though Shoeberg is dying. The reaction of the chief suggests much more strongly that Shoeberg is being an absolute pain in the ass.

Eventually Shoeberg recovers herself well enough to speak.

Shoeberg: I had some chilli that was defrosting, she says. Like, it was frozen from last November, but I'm not sure . . .

(Inaudible speech from Shoeberg now, as she coughs even more and jerks about, killing her lines dead. You wonder if the actor who plays the superior officer is going to break character and explode with rage. He looks actually furious about having to work with the actor playing Shoeberg. As if the wardrobe wasn't bad enough. You can see his eyes darting about, looking from face to face behind the cameras. They all know, too. Working with the actor who plays Shoeberg is a nightmare. Yet again, she is wasting everyone's time with this coughing that is not in the script.)

For the first time, you see Shoeberg front-on. She looks like a person who was destroyed long ago, and then, over many harsh years, she has had to glue herself back together again. Her face is shockingly thin. Her wilting eyes are the greyish colour of pebbles from a shingle beach. Hastings? Maybe St Leonards or somewhere. Her smile of gratitude is razor-tight as her superior shakes his head and hands her a few notes of cash from his own immense wallet.

Get it sorted, he says.

Yes, sir.

Today, Shoeberg.

Yes, sir.

Boss: And find me this bloody kid! He could be anywhere – even in a ditch. Have you checked all the ditches? I don't want an answer to that. I have already ordered a full-scale search of all the ditches within a twenty-five-mile radius of the boy's home *and* his *school*. It's taken a lot of manpower. A lot of overtime. Very expensive, so whatever you're actually planning on doing next, you'll have to do it alone. I've spent all the money.

Yes, sir.

There are no more resources.

Yes, sir.

No, in fact, I just remembered, you will not be completely alone. In fact, I want you to work with Simms. Simms is very bright, and incredibly organised and has told me personally that he despises you. He will be your partner.

Yes, sir.

Good. Now, there is one condition to Simms agreeing to work with you – and that's that you must not create any kind of stink or mess or bad atmosphere in his exquisite car.

You are drifting off a little now. Is any of this real?

Shoeberg nods, she raises her arms before getting herself to her feet, as though unable to fend off some physical, tendril-like presence of her superior officer's bullying jibes, or the unreasonableness of his requests, or his terrible policing.

Her mouth hangs open as she finally gets up to leave, pulling a big ugly shawl around herself. She grabs a shabby brown leather bag from somewhere near her feet and stuffs the cash directly inside it.

At her desk, in the busy police station, Shoeberg stares at the face of a young teenage boy who has obviously spent time as an army cadet. The missing boy. He is smiling and wearing a beret. His straw-blond hair and flushed cheeks speak of a healthy enthusiasm for military-type activities. Shoeberg sniffs and wipes her nose. On her desk is a large sub-type sandwich. It's a made-up brand, and you enjoy looking at the logo – which is two owl faces next to each other, drawn in gaudy red and brown lines.

The sandwich company is called SUB_OWL. The sandwich itself looks hugely inviting, a real achievement on the part of the edibles team in the props department. You actually want to eat the sandwich. You regret not cooking yourself any food, but just putting the grill on to high and then leaving it. You realise you haven't actually turned off the grill.

The grill is on in your kitchen.

But you want to see Shoeberg eat the sandwich. She reaches a hand out to it, she picks it up. She is so frail, you wonder if the sandwich will in fact eat her.

She opens her mouth strangely, appallingly wide, but just as she is about to finally eat something, Simms arrives. She pauses with the SUB_OWL just millimetres from her mouth.

Boss! He says. Boss – no time for snacking, I'm afraid. Payroll want to see you.

Now? Says Shoeberg. The actor playing Shoeberg really nails a mournful note here. Her yearning for that sandwich is palpable. The actor has probably not eaten anything for weeks. She has been preparing to truly mourn for that sandwich. She probably had many painful conversations with the edibles team in the props dept., telling the edible props assistant in detail how she was planning to starve herself, and swearing the assistant to secrecy while she took a near-suicidal plunge into starvation, just so this scene would work the way it does.

You can imagine the pained face of the edibles assistant, at home, not responding to his family who want to know how his big job in television is going. Ignoring his mother, who has put him up while he works as an unpaid intern for three years. Forcing himself to avoid food in solidarity with the actor playing Shoeberg, whom he secretly loves, and yearns to call sister.

You zone back into what's happening on screen. Simms is belittling Shoeberg further with some news he has about the payroll dept.

Patrice is after you, and he looks furious. Apparently someone told our superior officer that you didn't get paid?

Who told him that?

How should I know? But you shouldn't annoy that lot in pay-roll. Ruin your life, they can. If you get no-officed.

What's no-officed?

Ask Patrice, says Simms. He gestures in the direction of some other part of the office.

Shoeberg puts her sandwich down, rises ghoulishly from her seat, and leaves the shot, following the direction of Simms's outstretched hand into the distance. Simms, left alone with the massive, delicious-looking sandwich, picks it up. He sniffs it. He pulls an offended face. He chucks the sandwich in the bin.

There is a fifteen-second shot of the sandwich in the bin, nestled amongst balled-up A4 paper and loads of pencil shavings. Glistening chipotle sauce oozes like lava, mingles with bits of dust and collects in the ridges of the bin. A skein of ham slowly unfurls.

Now they're in a corridor. Maybe outside payroll? Patrice the payroll clerk is giving Shoeberg another bollocking. How dare you? he's saying. We paid you in full, into the bank account you gave us. And you go into a senior leader's office and lie about me! You question my professionalism at the highest level, without even a phone call?

Shoeberg looks pitiful, coughing, her shoulders rising and fall-ing, she is just bones. She says, But I didn't get any money. When I went to the bank, it took my card. I have nothing.

Well, you were probably so overdrawn that your entire salary didn't even get you back into the black.

I . . . I don't think so, that doesn't seem possible.

Patrice leans in very close to Shoeberg's face. You can tell he is probably a psychopath. You can imagine a future episode in which Patrice is revealed to have been the culprit in a spate of vicious attacks.

You are utterly pathetic, Patrice says. Everyone knows you can't even keep your head above water, despite being paid a good wage and having a tiny, cheap little flat. Everyone knows you're destitute because of your own shocking decision-making. And your tragic past is also a result of your feeble grasp of your life. I'm told you used to be a good detective, but there are plenty of people I would rather see in your job, all of them able to keep up with their DD payments. All of them capable of looking directly at their bank statement and seeing nothing to surprise them.

It's difficult, that's all. Listen, Patrice, please can you help me?

Yes, I can help you, says Patrice.

Oh thank god. Thank you, just a small advance is all—

Patrice stops her by raising a long, elegant hand. No, he says. I cannot help you like that. I can help you like this – look around you. Where are we?

In the corridor, says Shoeberg.

That's right, we're in the corridor. Not my office. Not your office. The corridor. This is an unofficial conversation. This is a chance for you to correct your mistake.

Oh.

Go and grovel to your superior officer. Make it clear you made a terrible mistake.

I can't – he's only interested in the case . . .

I don't think you have grasped the very precarious nature of the situation you're in, says Patrice. You are a corridor person now. Do you understand? Nobody will meet with you in an official place. Nobody will touch your files, your folders, overtime, equipment, expenses, your pension. You are a crack person. A gap. You are a person that doesn't technically even exist. Think about it. When was the last time anyone talked to you in their office?

Just now, I just came from—

Not police! Not police people! Real people. When was the last time an administrator had a conversation with you that wasn't next to the vending machine, or in the car park?

They just happened to catch me, that's all. It saves time . . .

Patrice raises his eyebrows. They are such meticulous eyebrows, they could in fact have been tailored for this exact expression. There is no word, you realise, for this experience. The experience of looking at someone's eyebrow and realising that you are subject to their power. This has happened to you in real life. You start thinking about this and then stop because of the action on the screen.

The actor playing Patrice is very gifted, but you realise that this role – immaculate administrative class with psychotic under-tones – is probably a type he gets cast as, with very little variation between jobs.

After he stops looking this immaculate, there is nothing for this kind of actor. You don't know his name. You wonder if you read somewhere that his body was found floating in the river, or that he filmed himself masturbating in the bath and sent it to his young assistant.

Patrice stares at Shoeberg with redoubled contempt. No, he is saying, no, they do not happen to catch you. They come to you in the corridors because they cannot stand to have you in their space, in their proper, official space. You do not belong, Ms Shoeberg. Try it, if you don't believe me. Knock on this door. Go on.

He gestures to the door they happen to be standing next to. 'B12' is all it says on the door.

Knock on door B12, says Patrice. And see if the people inside are willing to admit you.

B12?

Yes, B12. Do you even know what they do in there?

I . . .

The whole time Patrice is talking, Shoeberg has been fazing out. She looks pale. Her lips are blue. With great effort, she turns away from Patrice and staggers off, leaning on the walls as she goes, dragging herself across numerous informative posters (that have been designed from scratch by the excellent professionals in the props team).

Suddenly you remember you have left the grill on! You leap up and run into the kitchen, your heart is pounding. This is worse than the beetle! When you get there, you realise that you have left the grill on, but you actually didn't put any food on the grill.

You find a collection of the food things you have recently bought from the corner shop. You stand at the worktop and shove ham then white bread then ham then butter into your mouth. You chew and swallow just enough to allow room for more stuff. You ram in some Monster Munch crisps. You are panting with the ferocity of your own eating. You can hear shouting on the TV. Or sex. It could be either.

When you come back, for some reason, Shoeberg is at home.

Simms is drying himself with a ragged towel after taking a shower in Shoeberg's flat. He stalks into her bedroom, all skin and muscle and silhouettes of pubes. He tosses the towel onto the floor and languidly starts to get dressed.

Nobody can know about this, he says, pulling on a long, argyle-patterned sock.

Shoeberg nods absently. She's lying on her bare mattress, partly covered by a thin sheet. She blows a scrap of hair away from her face.

I need some money, Simms says.

What for?

To get my clothes washed, Simms says. I stink of sex.

Can't you just do that at home, she whispers.

Think about it for a second, Simms says. Just think about what you just said. Joan will notice, yeah? I need to get it done express. It's a lot of fucking around.

There is a silence while Shoeberg wrestles with the idea of giving this man her money.

It's in my bag, she says.

Ta.

He pulls all of Shoeberg's recently acquired money out of her brown satchel and puts it into his pocket. It is many, many times the amount required to wash Simms's clothes. She nods again, watching it go. Then, as Simms starts to leave, she sits up.

Wait! Where are you going? We still have to look for the missing cadet.

Simms grimaces. He's gone, Shoeberg. Why do you think we ended up doing that again?

I don't know.

Because he's dead.

He's not dead.

That cadet is dead and you needed to be consoled.

Shoeberg looks as though the effort of speaking is becoming too much. Her voice rattles as she adds, Please! And reaches out a hand towards Simms.

Simms does not disguise his revulsion. Now that he is clean, he wants to get out. Can't. Sorry. I have to go to the cake shop — wife's birthday. Special evening, etc.

There is a long silence. Simms looks at Shoeberg on the bed. He finally seems to show a shred of human decency.

Look, Shoeberg. Thank you for saving my life today. I'm sorry this er — whatever this is. I'm sorry because I know it's shit what I'm doing. I'm running away. I'm taking your money. I gave you pity sex. But I have to go. You can hate me if you want.

Shoeberg shrugs. She looks down at herself, under her little sheet.

Just go, she says.

Thanks. I'll save you some cake.

Actually, could you leave some of that money? It's been a while since I ate . . .

Simms is doing up his tie. Of course! He says. I'm not a total asshole. He winks without smiling. He leaves the door open as he goes out, without leaving any money behind.

Shoeberg lies alone in her bed for five minutes. The camera angles change so we can see every detail of her poverty as she goes over whatever happened with Simms in the bed, and presumably, whatever happened while you were eating crisps. Will she give you any clues about what led to her saving Simms's life? Is she any closer to saving the life of the missing cadet?

The camera agonises over her. Obsesses over her fingernails, her palms, her wrists, her wrinkled elbows, her one visible shoulder blade, her collarbone, her jaw. You wonder, will she stop breathing? Did the actor playing her collapse during the filming of this scene? She is so still, she could be dead. How long is left of the episode?

Then, with a gasp, she forces herself up, she struggles across the bed in her sagging underwear. Now she's making coffee in the kitchenette, letting a little street light come in through the window and fuzz up in the kettle steam. She nips at sugar from a spoon before putting it into the cup and stirring. She takes the coffee back to her bedroom.

Something has occurred to her, but there is no indication what it could be. Everything has happened while you were in the kitchen with your food and your failure to turn off the grill.

In fact, you should pay attention because the grill is still on and you are shrinking faster now than before. Soon you may not even be able to reach the controls for the grill.

Shoeberg is back on the bed, sitting cross-legged, she digs a file out of her massive brown satchel-type bag thing. You marvel again at the quality of the props department in this programme.

She lays out pictures of places and people you do not recognise, except one of them, you think, may have been an actor in the *Harry Potter* films. She analyses the pictures. She looks at them. Then she turns, leans away and stretches down the side of the bed. She returns with a scabby-looking laptop. She cannot connect to the internet.

Shit, she says. She pulls on a dressing gown.

She's outside the front door of a flat in her dressing gown. The door opens, a student stands in the doorway, she has hair in her face and a surly, educated arrogance in her smile. She looks poor at first glance, but in fact, looking closer, there are traces of money in her costume, in her posture. She is wearing a sort of mockery of Shoeberg's own dismal circumstances.

Peeping from beneath a pastel-blue M&S dressing gown is a classic X-Ray Spex T-shirt. The student's obvious hidden financial power makes Shoeberg hesitate.

Hi, I live upstairs. For some reason my internet isn't working. Can I er, I don't know the word, borrow your Wi-Fi?

The student shakes her head and sighs. Jesus, again? You still owe us from last time.

Sorry.

Fine. It's fifty quid though.

I'll give it to you next week – they're late paying me at work.

The student again shakes her head. She says Jesus. She looks at Shoeberg like she is a piece of shit.

You want the password?

Yes please.

OK, it's PatheticUpstairsLoserACAB.

All one word?

All one word.

Any caps?

Capital P on pathetic, U on Upstairs and L on Loser. ACAB is always all caps.

Thanks.

The student shuts the door in Shoeberg's face.

Shoeberg is back in her bedroom. She sits on her bed. She is looking at something on the screen. Her face is somehow full of hope, yet racked with the inevitable failure of whatever she's trying to do.

We see her typing the words Sycamore Plough into BLANDIT, a made-up search engine (this invented brand is nowhere near as subversive or clever as the SUB_OWL sandwich wrapping you saw earlier, but it's still pretty good. It's called BLANDIT DELIVERS and it has a picture of a kind of highwayman as its avatar. This is presumably a reference to the information superhighway. But you wonder if anyone else is going to get that reference. Also, it makes you think that this time the art department people have gone too far. Like, they have redefined what a search engine fundamentally is, just for the sake of this one scene – also you are shrinking you are absolutely shrinking to nothing. What will you do? If you could only get down from the sofa, but that feels impossibly far now. You consider trying to hypnotise a rat, would that work? You try to tell your family, or anyone, that you have downsized too far and things are really bad now and could someone come and help). Shoeberg clicks 'Deliver' and then the screen fills with results.

She clicks the top one and the shadowy faces of a group of men appear, they are walking through a dark car park – they seem to have been captured on CCTV outside a factory called Sycamore Plough. Music plays, insisting that this blurry image of shadowy men has some meaning to the programme, but you missed the relevance because you were in the kitchen stuffing crisps and milk into your mouth.

The lights go out in Shoeberg's room.

No, moans Shoeberg. Not now. Not this now.

But it's too late, the promise of those unpaid bills you saw earlier has been delivered upon. She's been cut off. She goes from room to pitch-black room, using the faces of the gang on her laptop screen as a kind of torch. Her flat in this light is a monstrous landscape. Her silhouette in the lounge is abject. She stands there, finally defeated by how shit everything is.

And then, rising up behind her in the gloom seems to be the hairy, grotesque shape of a monster/
BLEEEP BLEEEEP BLEEEEP YOU REALLY SHOULD HAVE TURNED OFF THE GRILL BLEEEEP BLEEEEP BLEEEP

Catmint

We all met at the agreed time, more or less. I was at the restaurant first, having walked quickly, and having had nothing to do before. My flat was tidy and bare. My work was done. The kids were with their mum.

Yes, I had walked quickly, but ought to mention that I had also taken a slight detour around Sycamore Park to look at the evening sun. It was a fabulous evening sun, set in a slow-dancing sky. Many colours – so many, and such rich pink, such emotional blue.

I had arranged for us to take the long feasting table that ran along the window. The window itself was a vast single panel. It was not tinted, and was so clean it almost vanished – it was as though there was nothing but a cushion of air and silence between the table and the busy street outside. The sky was enormous through this window, adorned with faint birds, like jewels in the distance.

I sat and admired this sky from my seat, alone at the head of the table, for a long time. I do not usually arrange events like this, and the vision of this sky and its faint birds, and the clean window, all helped me relax as the others – my great friends – arrived in drabs.

Each of them on arrival performed the same little routine: They came in, took a breath, looked around at the restaurant – which was dark and elegant and ran deep into a distance on all sides, giving the impression that the seating areas, the bar, the cocktail area, the coffee bar, the plinth of the maître d' were simply pools of light in a dark plateau. If you looked closely in those darker places, you would see that there were many details in the jet terrazzo floor, tapestries of moons slinked across the ceiling, light reflecting from raw metals picked out walls and banisters. I liked it anyway. So, they arrived, peered into the rich darkness, smiled at the occasional shimmers of brass, or flowing tapestries. Then they snapped out of it, accepted where they were, and began loosening their coats and handing them to waiters. Then they took another second or two to accept the atmospheric change now that they were no longer wearing outside garments. An odd sight, the way people seem to stop and receive messages from their skin. All over their body, their skin giving them messages about the temperature in this restaurant. I had never seen it before. And then they saw me.

Sylvester and Maude came first, looking well, bristling with expensive coats, both dark coats, but not charcoal, but not grey and not any kind of blue, but not black. I kissed them both as they took turns leaning over. Sylvester's cheek skin was incredibly soft, telling of hundreds of pounds of product, but no surgery, I think.

For a while it was the three of us, and I listened to Sylvester describing the sky.

'A wonderful sky,' he said. I agreed.

'Really I think such an emotional blue,' I said.

'Azure,' he said.

Sylvester and I continued to describe the sky, but he kept saying azure, and I didn't feel that Sylvester had adequately captured it, though I could not be specific about what he'd missed. Azure. I wasn't convinced by that at all, even though technically it was accurate.

Maude said she had been so worried about finding the place she hadn't been able to think much of the sky.

'But if I had to describe it,' she said, 'I would call it arresting. It certainly didn't help us finding this place.'

'It was fine finding the place!' Sylvester said. 'You make it sound like we're desperately late, darling, but we're the first ones here. We got a bit lost, but on an evening like this, it's a joy to be lost. It was fine. Fine,' Sylvester said.

'Yes, it was fine, because one of us was looking where we were going, and not staring at the clouds,' Maude said. She was smiling.

'There weren't any clouds, Maude,' Sylvester said. 'The sky was completely clear!'

'You wanker,' Maude said.

We all laughed and while we were laughing, in came Callum and Kevin looking well, smiling broadly, expanding their arms in a kind of synchronised display of air hugging, which then became real physical hugs.

I received my hugs graciously, first from Kevin – whose soft shirt collar pressed against my cheek, then from Callum, who was wearing a heavy sort of denim khaki jacket with heavy double breast pockets. The heft of one of these pockets landed on my forehead as he leant in. Somehow everyone who hugged me was at such an angle that some part of their clothing or skin ended up resting on the top of my head. I didn't manage to get all the way out of my seat before more came in – a great clump of them – Sally and Kim, John, Manuel, Tai and Morgan, and Charlotte who came alone and was last, but so welcome. All of them were such a welcome sight. Hot and flustered and glowing now as though we were all taking our place in a historical moment, but of course it was only dinner. Simply dinner.

I heard them speaking to one another – Tai and Morgan have a dog – 'The neighbour is on dog duty,' Tai says.

'Lucky you,' John says. 'I don't trust my neighbours at all. I had to put my dog in a kennel.'

Several of the others sympathised with John.

'We've all left people or dogs behind,' said Sally.

'Except us!' said Kim. 'We're both here!'

It went on like that, they were saying exactly the things I expected, these gorgeous people.

With all of them standing up, and myself still seated, I felt suddenly like an island. Charlotte and the other last arrivals looked unsure about making the trip up to my end of the table, such was the upheaval of seating and hanging coats and glancing into the dark, and feeling the scale of the darkness and the pools of light, and saying how nice it was and how hard to find. All of this formed a sort of barrier, and I still felt unable to stand, to go over and greet people on my feet, as I realised a true host should.

'It's awkward to keep leaning over people!' I said to Morgan, as he and I opted to wave before he took a seat at the far end of the table.

'Not for me!' Tai said, leaving Morgan's side to come round for the usual kisses on each cheek. He smelt of something expensive, I wondered if it was something new by Frederic Malle, or Byredo, but knew instantly this would be wrong. It would be a brand I had never heard of. He was gone before I could ask, I remained there, inside this brief world of Tai's body and fragrance while he went off again, immune to the barriers of the table, kissing everyone's cheeks, pressing their skin against his own, and radiating adventure, warmth and mischief.

We settled into things. I had pre-ordered some champagne for the table. I tried hard not to draw attention to the fact that it was champagne, not cava or prosecco, as a waiter went around, casually pouring glass after glass, and everyone drank heartily without acknowledging the fact it was champagne. Most of the glasses were emptied without anyone prompting a toast or a cheers of any kind. It was all very natural. You could argue that I should have raised a toast . . .

For my part, I drank my glass quickly, because I love champagne, and because I was not yet speaking to anyone at length. I did not have much to do. I was surveying the table, looking at my friends, and feeling happy that we had all made it and were together at last. I wanted to say this, to say how glad I was, but now everyone was hidden behind menus. Just beautiful, the menus, elegant paper, like silk, like shrouds.

Looking admiringly at the others, who were hidden, as I said, behind menus, I realised I had not managed to receive one from the waiter. The waiter had passed mine to Maude, who was annoyed by Sylvester's hogging of the one they shared.

'Bloody ridiculous,' I heard Manuel say, 'not enough menus.'

Someone else, I think Charlotte, handed him a spare that she had. 'Here you go baby,' she said. I wasn't sure if Charlotte even knew Manuel. I thought about asking why she was calling him 'baby', but for some reason it didn't seem like a good time to raise my voice. Also, I didn't myself have a menu.

I did not want to draw attention to my lack of a menu. What's a menu? Why worry? I told myself it was stupid to worry about menus. It was better that the menus we *did* have were so opulent that sharing was the natural way to go. A full set of these menus would be garish in fact. I had champagne, everyone was here and it was becoming a delightful evening outside.

Then Sylvester asserted himself.

Sylvester ordered appetisers, starters and main courses for himself and Maude. It sounded like a sound choice, so I copied them. It was all the seafood options. Scallops, bisque, trout, samphire, crémant sauce which sounded interesting. I planned to deviate from them later on, and have a chocolate-based dessert, which I knew they would not do on any account. Sylvester would order something stodgy and custardy, and Maude would have coffee and go outside to smoke. It was fine. I knew this would happen and it was so lovely to know my friends so well and to accept them, consciously accept them for who they were.

Sylvester objected to chocolate on schoolboy principles. You didn't have chocolate at his school. Sweets were either boiled or chews. Dessert was white, yellow and red. Chocolate was somehow for mothers only or, at a push, sisters and aunts. Sylvester! I didn't even know how he and I managed to stay friends. But we did. We did.

I drank more champagne. I signalled to the waiter to bring just one more bottle. I did some maths and reasoned the cost of additional champagne could be absorbed by the taxi fare I would surely not spend, not tonight, when the evening was so beautiful, and I would have the energy for a walk, I felt sure.

Sylvester was talking loudly, but I didn't really understand what he was saying. He was the focus for a while. He looked well on it. I admired him already, of course, and had done since Maude first introduced him to us. But he looked especially well this evening. His crisp white shirt opened pleasantly onto his neck. His neck was wide and muscular and tanned. And he was so confident when he ordered all this fish for himself and Maude, and me, with such conviction. I told myself I was glad he was at my end of the table. Down the other end, Morgan said something salacious that I missed, but everyone down there was laughing. Tai was affronted as usual and dismissed Morgan's comments with a wave of his hand.

Tai saw me watching this and rolled his eyes. 'Champagne!' he shouted.

'That's right!' I shouted back.

Me and Tai cheersed in the air. I felt amazing. Everyone else also cheersed in the air, then went back to their conversations.

After a lull, I asked Maude how she was doing in her new job.

'Well, it's been a bit of a rollercoaster!' she told me. 'But my boss is so lovely.'

'Ah,' I said. 'That's so important. A good boss.'

'Yes, she's lovely. She's twenty-eight!'

'Wow,' I said. 'It's so good that you're happy.'

We didn't get much further than this because someone – it was John – started laughing very loudly. It'd been ages since I saw John, so his laugh had not yet become annoying, or oppressive as it used to. Do I mean oppressive? Perhaps that's unfair, it was just his laugh. I loved it actually, hahaha-haha-hahahaha – that's how it went. The same laugh every single time. The same volume, the same flat delivery. I loved hearing it, though in the past, as I say, I had felt heavily oppressed by it.

I drank more champagne and focused on my breathing for a while. The expense is fine, I said to myself. Let it go. The tablecloth is really clean and lovely. The glasses for water are really unique. After a pleasant interlude spent like this, absorbing the convivial sound of friends catching up, without having to play any particular role, food started to arrive. Heaps and heaps of food. I had no idea who had ordered all this food. I reeled as I realised I really ought to have a handle on all this, since I would be picking up the bill.

Then I calmed myself. I listened to my breathing. It would be fine. There was plenty in the other account. If I sneaked into the overdraft, it would be all right. I allowed plates to be pushed my way. I waded in.

I ate in a kind of trance. The food was just so good, so much butter and salt. Sauces, just everything was sauces. I recall some long moments while I held bread and butter in my mouth, the perfect balance of texture, fat and salt felt like a new kind of purity. It felt holy in some way. The rest of the party was doing the same, just eating in this amazing trance right through appetisers, right through starters. We ate bread and golden olive oil. More wine came, which was interesting, but not champagne.

I drank a lot of rosé that Sylvester said he had ordered, on the recommendation of Manuel.

Outside, the cars swam by in glistening clean shoals.

The sky was the same as it had been when we arrived, I noticed, even though we had been there for an hour or so.

'I can't take my eyes off that sky,' I said to Sally, gesturing to the bright world outside the huge clean window pane. Sally didn't hear me because someone dropped their knife onto their plate. 'It is an evening sky, isn't it?'

I was trying to say dusk, but for some reason, it couldn't be said. *Dusk.* I could probably say it now, but of course now is far too late. I tried again, but someone dropped a knife again.

'What did you say?' Sally asked. She seemed in pain from the sound of the dropped knife. I think it was Manuel who dropped his knife. He shrugged instead of saying sorry, but then he smiled his massive gorgeous smile, and Sally smiled back. I mentioned the sky again, but she didn't really register. She looked outside and seemed to agree with me, but didn't manage to quite articulate much.

I tried one last time to strike up a conversation, but in the general sound of eating and murmuring, my voice, the frequency of my voice, became lost. I forgot about it. The noise was not irritating, it was the sound of us all together again for the first time in years, I was so happy. I felt the warmth that only friendship can bring you. I felt that warmth flooding me, sluicing away all abstract notions of cost, and of debt. Of this strange feeling of being in trouble that life seemed to be giving me. I ate more. I ate and ate over all my unsaid things.

I ate so much bisque I worried I would not manage the trout. I ate three or four more of those religiously good bread rolls too, heaped with butter. I ate with gusto, and nobody else was holding back either. A meal after being starved, is how it felt to me. I thought maybe it was the same for everyone. The cars sailed by silently, without end. Someone said something about a painting they had seen recently. I heard the words describing this painting and for a moment I felt like I was standing in front of it. I could see the way the clouds dominated the sky, and the people in the distance seemed at once heroic and painfully alone and insignificant. I could see the chips in the golden frame. I could see the river, the harbour, the ships, the city with its spires. I was lost in this feeling that I had to go to the gallery and see this painting, even though I never go to galleries, and seeing paintings usually makes me feel tired, and like I have missed out on an important lesson at school, and I feel a strong need to move on and yet at the same time to sit down or get into a car and be driven away.

I looked outside.

The sky was the same. It hadn't changed even though now fully two hours had passed, it was the same deep blue. Rich pink. Motionless clouds.

'What an evening!' I said. 'What a sky!' I said it generally because at this time – when the sides that went with the mains were not yet finished, but imminently would be – I knew we had reached the stage where nobody would have time for any mean-ingful interaction with me before the evening came to an end. It was over, that's how it felt, and I had barely said a word to anyone.

'What an evening,' I said again. 'What a sky.'

Nobody replied, but it didn't matter. They had come. Everyone was here because I had invited them, and they had thought, Yes, I will go to this evening with him. I will do that. I had planned it very carefully.

Everyone had someone to talk to, as I had planned. They were each in pairs, except Charlotte who never seemed to need a second person and would always prefer to be alone and sort of float through things.

So everyone had someone, except, I realised, I did not have someone. Not such careful planning after all, because I had forgot-ten to give myself someone to talk to.

When I said, 'What an evening, what a sky,' it was heard only by the bones of the trout. The shocked dry eyes of its old head. I ate some chives and potatoes and forgot about it. I ate a spicy parsnip and several forks of baked harissa kale. I ate in a dream, all these sides, I don't remember asking for any of it, but the dishes continued to come my way, handed one after another by my dear friends. I ate doggedly, full of joy. I saw more being ordered but allowed these visions to be simply a blur, I was beyond worrying about the bill.

'Maude, tell us more about your boss,' I said loudly, almost shouting, when the mains were finally gone, and I was waiting for my chocolate pudding. Maude said she didn't want to talk about that any more. Quite a few of the people at the table seemed appalled that I would bring it up. I apologised. Then I raised my glass.

'Cheers!' I said. 'Here's to all my wonderful friends!'

'Cheers!' everyone said. We all clinked glasses, it took a while. I turned back to the window. The sky had remained the same. I wanted to discuss this with someone, but I could also see that it was a very boring subject. The cars floated by like swans. I watched them for a while, and fell into a state of waiting. The cars moved in near-silence, the sound of their passing occurring inside my head, a faint purr added in by an unconscious editor.

When I turned back to the table, chocolate pudding had arrived. I ate automatically, like a basic early Earth organism clos-ing over its nourishment, moving through layers of nougatine, praline, noisette, ecstatic crisp membranes of tempered chocolate.

When it was gone, I came back to myself, as though coming out of a trance. Sylvester was addressing one of the waiters. He seemed to be lecturing the poor guy.

I realised Sylvester was taking over now. He was fully assuming control of my evening. I found it unsettling, but that was classic Sylvester. Hadn't I known he would do this when I invited him? Even my ex had said it was a mistake to invite him. 'You know how he gets,' she'd said, after the kids had said their goodbyes and vanished into her house, to their preferred bedrooms, and their preferred snack cupboard. 'It pisses you off so much,' she had said. 'The way Sylvester is all the time.'

I'd held up my hands and said something about needing Maude to be there, and she refused – was unable to come without him –

which was true, she never went anywhere without Sylvester. And Maude needed to be there, otherwise what was the point?

There was a moment where I felt sure that my ex-wife would have wanted to say something like, 'What's the point indeed?' – meaning this whole thing was an expensive joke really – but she never did. So perhaps we had both grown since the divorce.

Instead, my ex-wife said of Maude, 'She could make an effort to come alone. She could leave Sylvester at home for once. After all, Maude knows better than anyone how impossible Sylvester is. How much he likes to take over.'

I'd held up my arms and I said she was right and what could I do and so on. In truth, I would have said anything to avoid letting the conversation turn to the cost of the evening. Anything to avoid the cost of the evening, and then what I owed her, and then over and on to how we came to be like this. I do not remember, I would have wanted to say, how it came to this. Why do my children live here now? Whose shoes are those in the entrance hall to this house? I don't remember, I would have wanted to say. I don't remember and I am sorry for whatever I did. I am so confused and sorry.

I will keep up my side, I would have had to say. I will pay my end of the kids' needs. But surely, after all that has slipped away from me, surely I can be allowed to take my friends out for an evening, can't I? After all they have done for me over the years. Surely, after all they have done for us? The many times I have been rescued rose up then to me at the table, a blur of guilt and relief and gratitude and guilt again.

As I continued to drift away into this unhelpful conversation that I had, in any case, avoided, I failed to notice Sylvester ordering a number of extravagant spirits and cocktails and coffees, all the while waggling his platinum card in the air, and declaring he would take care of all of it – nobody had to lift a finger, he wouldn't hear of it, waggling his shimmering fish of a card through the air, but of course, I would still pay. I would still pay for it all. Maude would intervene or Sylvester would forget the PIN for that silver card of his. I would still have to pay for all this but I didn't care. Hadn't I earnt one night where I pay? Hadn't my friends done their bit over the years?

I reasoned that if I split it between two or even three credit cards, I could spread the cost easily over four months without too much impact. If a waiter would let me come with them to the till or somewhere secluded, I could avoid the humiliation of the others seeing the bill, and of seeing me select which cards could cover the cost. I was thinking I could probably reduce the payments on one or two loans – just for a month. And then I would still be able to treat the kids, as I had promised, the next weekend. I would not let them down. I never had.

'Did I hear you correctly?' I asked, suddenly coming to my senses. 'Sylvester! Did you just ask for beds?'

'Yes!' Sylvester said. 'Beds all round!'

The waiters brought beds – beds on wheels of brass. Double beds for the couples. A king size for Sylvester, which he slapped with his wallet-shaped hands, single beds for the singles, which for the evening included me.

'Bedtime you tired old fuckers!' Morgan shouted.

I saw that Morgan and Tai and the others were piling into a colossal conjoined bed of beds. They were carrying bottles of champagne that had been brought by the waiters. I did not know who ordered them. I let it go. So what? I thought, and again, can't I just treat my friends?

'Bedtime!' Sylvester shouted. He leapt into his bed like a salmon.

'Bedtime!' I, too, shouted. They had wheeled out my bed last, and on seeing it, I realised that I was among friends and that was exactly, exactly where I had wanted to be, and that it was worth all the money in the world.

'Bedtime!' I shouted.

'Bedtime!' shouted everyone else, though with less vigour, it seemed, this time around.

As I settled into my bed, I felt again the distance between me and the tangle of the main group. I could hear them laughing and swooning magnificently into their beds. Morgan was calling someone a hag and they were all laughing. He was calling someone a trollop and they were all laughing their heads off.

Gradually it died down to more conventional muttering and the giggling shift of blankets as people huddled together in the mega bed. Nearer me Sylvester and Maude, more adult as usual, were applying cream from a tub to their faces. A waiter was holding the tub of cream for them.

'Have some face cream!' Sylvester said. 'It's amazing. It will take years off you.'

I applied some of the face cream. The waiter who held it for me smiled as I scooped from the tub, uncertain about how much to take. What was the right quantity? I tried to get it right. I rubbed it on, but could not stop looking at the waiter as I did so, using his face as a kind of mirror. The waiter, while I did this, kept his mouth locked in a polite smile. I examined his face. There were small smooth patches on his cheeks where he was wearing some kind of make-up. I felt anxious that I wasn't applying the cream properly. The waiter smiled encouragingly. I rubbed more of the cream onto my skin. It felt somehow tingly, like tea tree or eucalyptus.

'Is this eucalyptus?' I asked.

'Catmint!' shouted Sylvester, who had it slathered down to his collarbone.

'Catmint?'

'Catmint!'

The cars swished by like enchanted babies. I lay back in the sweet comfort of my single bed. I was absorbed into fresh sheets, seemingly endless crisp layers of blankets, each subtly quilted, lightweight.

I heard the whispered conversations of the others from my bed, even as I was trying to get to sleep. I worried about how much it was all costing. I had money that needed to be sent to my ex's account. The kids needed clothes for the new school term. It would be typical if I ended up being unable to meet my responsibilities because of something as decadent as sleeping in a restaurant. I put it out of my mind. Long ago – around the time I allowed Sylvester to order me extra cheese – I decided I would pay with the emergency credit card.

It had been a wonderful evening, I reminded myself. And the sky – the relentless blue sky had not aged at all. We slept under the protection of nets. Nets and laser-activated insect repellents. Yes, we slept in happy comfort. Every worry that came – the debt I was in already, the failure of my marriage and the tired distance in the eyes of my son – his almond-shaped blue eyes – my daughter's silence – all of them came as usual in waves, but my restaurant bed, my wine-filled skin rolled away from them. Whatever happened, they knew I loved them. Whatever happened, they would never go without. Not like their mother and I went without. Money was coming of course, and it was fine. Sylvester was snoring and a waiter came to gently apply a safety clamp to his epiglottis. The safety clamp was the shape of a swan. Someone came to my bed, another waiter, a senior member of staff, and very calmly leant over my body and activated the noise-cancelling feature of my bed.

'Oh sorry,' I said. 'I didn't realise.'

The waiter couldn't hear me of course, and went away in silence. Other people dining at nearby tables occasionally looked over at me under my blanket and I smiled at them. An elderly couple, in their pastel best, bent low to me and smiled. It was clear from a bulging tote bag under their table that they had come prepared with pyjamas and eye masks, and were excited to have done with the cheese so they could get into bed too.

After the initial excitement and arrangements of the beds, I felt lonely for an hour or so. I could not tell how everyone was doing. Kevin, for example, had barely spoken to me. He was sleeping just one bed over, on the other side of Sylvester and Maude. I assumed he was fine. But I had been meaning to speak with him, to engage him in a long conversation about his life and work. I whispered his name, thinking maybe he would hear me – like he might pick the sound out above the general ambient sounds of sleeping and noise-cancellation noise.

'Kevin, have you noticed the sky?' Of course, he didn't respond to this. He waved a lazy hand – not towards me – but at something unseen, a passing dream, and he broke out into a wide old smile at the ceiling.

Like everything else that had tried to assail me, the sky was washed away, it was beautiful. Also beautiful was the vision of Kevin waving. His happy huge smile.

I slept on soft waves. I visited a harbour in my dream. I became tiny.

I woke to the sound of kettles boiling and the fragrance of strong coffee. A waiter had come and turned off the noise cancellation around my bed. We were all given newspapers – heavy, luxurious newspapers with endless features and crosswords and glossy pages that slipped all over my quilts. I read an extended interview with a celebrated Dutch goalkeeper from the 1990s, who now works for a foundation in Alaska. He spends his time out there measuring quantities of snow in a particular area of Alaska. The snow is melting, of course, but the former goalkeeper says there is so much hope. As much hope as snow, he says.

It was a really interesting article, I was still reading it at the table, after the beds were taken away and I had been escorted back to my place.

'I should find a waiter and settle up,' I said, after a fourth cup of coffee, but nobody heard me. Sylvester and Maude were on the final clue of the hard cryptic crossword. I asked for the clue, but was told there's no way I'd get it. 'Trust me,' Maude said. 'It's a bollocks one. It'll be Latin or something or a poem by Browning.'

I let the crossword clue go. I was too relaxed and rested to get into it. I was good at crosswords, but not that good.

I felt sleepy. A good kind of groggy.

'I should get the bill,' I said to Sylvester.

'Not yet, chap,' he said.

All at once, we were back into it, all at the table, all talking in hushed, loving tones. We got three courses for breakfast. The cars outside the window were scootching by like musical notes.

The sky was as obstinately beautiful as before – I said to my friends, 'Look at the sky!'

'We know!' came a voice from down the table. I couldn't see who it was, but most people laughed.

I noticed that several of the group had changed their clothes. I looked at Sylvester, he was wearing a similar ensemble to the night before, but his shirt was now blue. His cologne was intoxicating. I swallowed bacon, hash browns, toast.

'Sylvester, have you had a shower?'

'Hours ago, matey!' he said. 'You were sleeping. Not to worry, you can have one after the walk.'

'A walk?' I said. I wasn't sure about a walk.

'Yes, we have to go for a walk!' Kevin was speaking now. 'I've arranged it all. We are going for a walk.'

I couldn't react to this news. A walk? I was so deep into the experience of the baked beans, and then, as they were taken away, juices were brought, more coffee. I ate muesli. I had a poached egg with hollandaise and smoked salmon. It was on a muffin. Royale, I was eating a royale. Sylvester, Maude, Kevin, and Charlotte were mulling over kedgeree. I had peppered fish paste on toast. I had snarling black coffee. I had a Danish pastry, I had pain au chocolat. It seemed it would never end.

A waiter came with boots and jackets, quilted jackets. I let the waiter dress me.

'This way!' It was Kevin now, taking over. Sylvester and Maude were more insular, enjoying each other. Sylvester had his hand in Maude's hand. She had her head near his head. I couldn't see past them, I could only hear the general willingness to go for a walk, and see the single shape of Maude and Sylvester as we stumbled into the expensive gloom of the restaurant.

I saw, as I walked by, that the elderly couple were still asleep. Their eyes twitching, and the sharp jags of their pupils rolling under their eyelids. I hushed my group, but they didn't hear. I pulled an apologetic face at one of the waiters. He smiled and shook his head, They can't hear you, he was saying. They have their noise cancellation activated.

We pressed on through the restaurant, emerging into the car park out the back. It was a drab, grey zone of dust and damp. No concrete to be seen – it resembled an abandoned building site. The walls at the far end looked strange, uneven white mortar and steam. I looked back towards the restaurant. A couple of the waiting staff were leaning against the cracked white wall of the building. They looked absolutely dead-on-their-feet exhausted. They smoked, did not acknowledge us.

'Where are we walking?' I asked Kevin.

'This way!' he said. He headed towards the far end of the car park. We followed, I expected to be on St Anne's Road, which leads towards the park and, eventually, to my flat.

But somehow Kevin, directed by a member of the waiting staff, veered off to the right, towards the dirty high wall that enclosed the car park. As we approached, I jostled to try and get a sense of where we were heading. I could just make out a small brown door

– like the door to an ancient shed, or a lean-to. A hard shrivelled door that creaked as Kevin opened it.

'Oh yes!' someone shouted – I believe it was Tai.

'Dooooor!' chimed Charlotte.

I could feel in the air that everyone was gripped with excitement as we funnelled, single file, through the door.

In the reshuffling process I managed to slip in front of Maude and Sylvester, who I now sensed in the tight alley space behind me, shuffling, making sounds of approval. I could have been wrong, but it sounded as though Sylvester was eating grapes as he walked. Yes, in fact, I realised they were all eating grapes. Round perfect emerald grapes. The fragrance of the grapes was all-encompassing – every few seconds I had the feeling I was within the skin of one of these grapes, a stretched-out skin, taut to balloon proportions, surrounding me and then evaporating with a pop. The grapes were being handed out to people by hands emerging from the alley walls.

Silver trays appeared, offered from shuttered windows, they seemed to appear at the wrong moment for me, I could not see what was on them, I flinched when they appeared. I was growing claustrophobic in the narrow brick-lined passage. They were simply drinks of course, drinks on trays that appeared from the windows.

Up ahead, I saw my companions collecting vials of pastel-coloured liquids. They were like milkshakes in laboratory vials, but not thick milkshakes at all. Very thin. The way I would make milkshakes for my children at home, without ice cream or any of that faff, just syrup and ice-cold milk.

Soon the alleyway opened up and we were in a grassed, walled garden. I had come to expect these things by now, and spread out in front of us was a vast picnic blanket, pure white, upon which were platters of fruit, buckets of ice with champagne and more serious-looking whites and rosés. Crude wooden crates contained fresh bread. There were hints of other things too, bowls of delicate salads. On a small table, tilting at a wild angle, were ranged iced jugs of summer cocktails. There was a stick in the ground near a rosemary bush covered in syrup to draw away the wasps.

There were a lot of wasps on the stick, and a member of the waiting staff who seemed to be whispering to the wasps in a discouraging way.

'We can't be eating again!' I said. Everyone in the group turned to look at me, as though they had forgotten I existed.

Someone threw a grape at my head. I couldn't see who it was.

'Beds!' Charlotte shouted.

Beds were wheeled over the grass, coming from large gates in the vast garden wall. They emerged from beneath the climbing roses, pushed by waiting staff from the restaurant that was no longer visible or possible to conceptualise.

I tried to ask the waiter who brought my bed if they could tell me how much the bill currently stood at. I had abandoned the maths at this stage and was already resigned to the fact I would have to get at least one new credit card in order to move the money. I had left my phone in my coat, I realised, and so could not apply for one online.

I climbed into the bed and lay looking at the sky. Still those blues, those clouds, those pinks – these poetic beings sailing across the sky. Everything was silent. The wasps flew like swans around their stick.

'This sky,' I said. 'I just can't believe the sky!'

'We know!' the others shouted. They shouted it all at once.

'We know about the sky!' Sylvester and Maude were the first ones at my bed, at the foot of the bed, but soon I was surrounded by them, all of them looking down upon my body, and I was so tired suddenly.

'I'm sorry,' I said. 'I can't eat anything else for a while. I need to rest.'

Someone's hand was on my foot – it was Morgan, who is very kind to me in these moments when things are at an end.

'Maude,' I said. 'I did so mean to catch up with you more.'

Maude, who was at the top end of the bed, nodded. Then she shook her head. Everyone was laughing.

Someone opened more champagne and then everyone was on the bed, they were climbing onto my chest. I had a glass of champagne in my hand and was trying to drink it but they were continuing to climb on my chest and the glass felt further away and less necessary.

I looked at the sky and they were crushing the breath from me, and I have never felt more shocked by a sky.

Sonic Gold

I have come to visit Jon. After all these years, he still does repairs above Bard's Audio, the music shop on the corner where Gosling Lane meets the High Street. There used to be the big Gateway's supermarket next door, but it's gone now.

Jon calls his repairs service Sonic Gold, but I don't think it's actually registered as a business or anything. The little sign that points up the stairs from the main shop just says 'Repairs and Collections'.

The workshop is the same as always. The air smells dry, of hot wires and carpet tiles. The workspace is neat but not fussy – the hanging plastic handles of his little pliers are still in line – sage green, black, red, in order of size. The tools are old, but seem cared for.

I've never seen him actually mend anything. He seems to only work for about an hour a day. I don't know what he does with the rest of the time he spends here. Probably he just sits, having his thoughts. I've spent evenings in his car with him, just smoking, saying nothing, paused in the lay-by, looking at the dark road ahead of us.

I imagine he is like that – his pale blue eyes looking out at the plastic and metal, blinking away cigarette smoke and sipping coffee. He prepares this coffee in the little back room that I have only been allowed in once. Jon is very specific about boundaries in the shop. I'm not even really meant to use the toilet here.

Jon usually has a huge science fiction book on the go, the covers faded blue and pink, slab-like books that were never resting far from his hand. I've always wanted to catch him in the act of reading, but never have.

It's the late end of what I'd call mid-morning. I came here an hour ago, unannounced, just as I used to. Outside the sun is shining against the flash of a recent shower. We started talking naturally, falling into our usual routine. I told him my news – kids are well, Em is enjoying having her own company. He seemed to take it in, reminded me how lucky I was, etc. And then we moved on to his life. I asked how his mum was doing.

'She's losing her hair,' Jon told me.

'Oh that's not good! Is it connected to anything else? I mean, anything more serious.'

'No.' Jon spread peanut butter on another chocolate digestive biscuit. 'It's stress. Her landlord.'

'That prick again?'

'Mmm.'

There has been a damp problem in the flat since we were kids. Over the years, I've helped Jon repaint the walls in her bedroom with mould-proof paint at least four times. I've also helped him install some industrial-strength dehumidifiers. I've gone with him to the landlord's to talk things through.

He takes me along to help with these things, he has said, because his mother trusts me. She trusts me to explain clearly what's going on, which Jon struggles with. He has the same issue with his customers. He has stopped giving diagnoses when hi-fis are brought in. He just tells them the cost and how long to fix it. It seems to work OK.

What we like to do is eat chocolate digestive biscuits with smooth peanut butter spread across the top. We are doing this now. We leave his mother for now, and move on to preparing more biscuits. We do four at a time. More than this feels gluttonous.

'Hey Jon,' I say. 'What's that?'

I'm pointing down at the corner of the little workshop area behind Jon's foot. His dry foot, with its purple heel that bulges out the back of his sandal like a brain.

'What's what?' Jon asks me. He doesn't acknowledge that I am pointing at a sleek black briefcase with gold clasps, smooth black leather, down there on the floor.

The briefcase reminds me of films in which the main character has to deal with a smug business adversary who carries a sharkish black briefcase exactly like the one next to Jon's foot.

'Anyway, it might rain,' Jon says. 'So I mean there will have to be something put up. You can talk to her neighbours about that. I know the woman at 6B has one, because we lent it to her last year. She's still got it or she has thrown it away. If she's thrown it away, she'll have to get a new one anyway. She can get one at Dyas. They do them for £60.'

'One what?' I ask.

'Gazebo.'

'A gazebo?'

Jon raises an eyebrow at me, as though I am supposed to understand what he is talking about.

'You want me to tell the woman at 6B to buy a gazebo if she hasn't still got her old one?'

'Well, we'll need more than just that one. Three at least.'

'Three gazebos? Jon, I'm lost on the gazebos here.'

Jon sighs and repeats what he has said about the possibility of rain and the need for gazebos. In the meantime, I happen to glance down again under the desk, just in time to see Jon's foot daintily move in front of the briefcase and slide it out of sight.

'But you have to erect them quite late in the process, or at least don't make too much noise, in case Mum sees. If she sees that we're putting up gazebos, she will start getting stressed. Better if it's a surprise.'

'Yeah OK, a surprise party. Is that what we're talking about?'

'Yes, we'll tell her about it but casually. A surprise, but not a shock.'

Jon keeps going in this vein, unravelling his thoughts. There's no point in mentioning that I didn't know about this party, and I don't know when it is or if I can be there, or if I am available to help.

'Don't you think she'd like more time to get ready,' I suggest, 'I mean, if she's got the alopecia to deal with?'

Jon shakes his head at me like he's talking to a child.

'No no, she'll already have a hat or a scarf on because she will have been told she's getting taken for lunch.'

'Right, but then instead of going out for lunch, she'll just be downstairs in the communal gardens?'

'Communal gardens, exactly.'

'No worries, Jon. I can help sort the gazebos. I think we will be lucky with the weather.'

Jon's face relaxes. I hadn't planned to come in and see him so who knows how he was planning to get all this sorted, but it's obvious that his mother's alopecia situation was only a side shoot, a tendril of the real thing on his mind which is this birthday party. 'When is it, Jon?' I ask. 'When is the party?'

'Two p.m. tomorrow.'

'Woah!' I say. 'OK, no worries, I'd better get started with the gazebos, but I really don't think it will rain too badly, if at all. If we can't get any it will be fine still, I think.'

'No,' he says, looking not at me, but at some point on his desk. 'We need them.'

'But if we can't, I'm saying. If we can't, it'll still be OK.'

Ignoring the gazebos, Jon moves on to food, which also has not been sorted.

'Safeway's has a sale on,' he says. 'Barbecue two for one. Deli counter three for ten quid.'

'Right. I guess I can help with the shopping too. Do you have a list?'

'No list.'

'OK no problem. What does your mum like?'

'She likes nibbles,' he says. 'She likes all the sides, you know?'

'Sure, I know.'

'Can you get Panang chicken from the deli counter. Maybe some steaks and some sticky marinade – they do liquid smoke marinade now,' he says.

'Oh great,' I say, 'That saves a lot of time I guess.'

'Well no. Actually, it's not smoky enough for me. The liquid smoke company themselves make the marinade, but I add more LS' – he actually says 'LS' in place of 'Liquid Smoke' – 'to it. So get brown sugar and soy sauce to add to the existing premade marinade. It really lifts it.'

'Sounds amazing,' I say. I'm looking at that briefcase again. I detach myself from Jon's voice, tethered by the idea that he's still describing the marinade requirements for the steaks. I'm looking at his purple heel again, bobbing up and down as he talks. It looks like he will kick the briefcase over, but he doesn't quite ever make contact with it. I want to press him again on this briefcase, but I realise he is now talking about guacamole. He's describing the table layout, ' . . . snacks, dips, your guacamole, obviously, bread, fucking chopped carrots or whatever.'

'Wait, you want me to make guacamole?' I ask.

'Of course! Your guacamole! The one you make. Your guacamole that you won't let anyone call "guac".'

'I don't think I have a guacamole, Jon. And with everything else, maybe I shouldn't really commit to too much prep.'

Jon gives me a sympathetic look, as though I have forgotten something very simple.

'You made it before,' he says. 'At the last one.' The last one was probably her fiftieth birthday, so a decade ago. 'She really likes your guacamole.'

My guacamole is really just mashed avocados with salt, coriander and lime juice. I'm not even sure it technically passes for guacamole because it has no onions in it. It's meant to have raw onion in it, I feel sure of that. I feel convinced that true guacamole is literally just a raw onion mashed into four to five avocados. You add some salt and pepper and lime and coriander leaves. I think about true guacamole for a while, I gaze at the exposed soft paper cone of a woofer (subwoofer?) that has been dismantled over in the corner of the workshop. When I return to the conversation, Jon is listing crisp flavours he wants to get.

'Have you sent out reminders and everything?' I ask him. 'Who's coming?'

He gives me his phone. 'Look for a group called "Silvia's Party".'

'Right, OK.'

I eventually find the group in amongst some chats that seem to be with angry customers, complaining about how long it's taking for their audio equipment to get fixed. A lot of them say things like 'Really regret ever trusting you. How long will it be then?' etc. One of them says, 'You have ruined my daughter's wedding. You promised it would be ready, and you let us down. Watch your back, m8.'

I try my best to send out a message to the family group as if it is coming from Jon himself. Jon texts in this enthusiastic language that does not match his usual voice or his manner. This is my impression of him:

Hey everyone! Super excited to see you at the party tomorrow. Mum is really looking forward to seeing you all. X

'Sent,' I tell him. 'All good.'

'What time did you say? It's changed.'

'Oh – I er – I didn't say a time. Did you not already tell them?'

'No. It's changed.'

'Right. No worries, tell me the time. And I guess I can confirm where it is too. Do they know where?'

'Yeah at Mum's obviously in the communal garden.'

'I'll just reiterate the place. No harm in hammering it home. So what time?'

'People will want to watch the match so they should get in early.'

'OK, what time is the match?'

'Hmm.'

'Shall I put three? That's the normal time, isn't it?'

'Put five.'

'OK, five.'

Hey everyone! Forgot to say, please come to Mum's at 5 p.m. The footy will be on earlier for those who want it, then we will be in the communal garden for summer evening nibbles and food.

I sweat a little over the word 'footy'. Jon's brothers can be quick to berate him about such things.

'Do they say "footy"?' I ask, but Jon doesn't reply.

Sometimes it's better not to press him on these things. He's really not interested in football. It's for his brother Darren's benefit, and the other men in his mother's life, the ones who live in the same flats and share the gardens. She likes them to come to hers for the match, always has. She never watches it.

The first time I went to Jon's home, the football was on. We were probably fourteen years old. His older brother, and his usual five friends, all heaving in the living room, occupying every inch of space. Dirty jeans on the deep pile rug, bottles of beer on every surface, those 1.5-litre bottles of Corona, one per male, with spares in bags at their feet, the smell of recent childhood turned bitter.

Jon's father had gone not long before. Jon hadn't mentioned it much, but I knew his brother had taken it badly. Had cut himself with a severed ashtray outside the Royal Oak. The scar, a livid slug, bulged out of his forearm, little hyphens growing out of it from the staples they put in to stop the bleeding.

Jon and I were ignored as we picked our way to a patch of carpet and watched solemnly as the game played out on the screen. Only Jon's mother paid us any attention, making the bigger boys pass along little stubby bottles of French lager for us.

'Someone's got to drink them!' She said, opening the complicated flap on the cardboard box. 'There's hardly any alcohol in them anyway, which is why Darren won't touch it! You boys enjoy the game, don't let them take up all the space.'

The game itself was intensely boring. The farting and shouting in the room was unbearable, and by half-time, when the brother and his friends all got up to smoke and piss and scratch, I asked Jon if we could skip the rest of the match. I pleaded with him, but he was adamant we stay and watch until the end. Before anyone else came back in, Darren returned to the room. He didn't speak, but mounted Jon, putting his full weight on top of Jon's back, shoving his head down to the carpet, beating him and kicking him in the ribs, and then sort of humping him and punching his head.

I felt a cold weight in my stomach, like if I'd swallowed one of those little bottles of beer whole. It happened as though I wasn't even there.

Jon didn't try to stop it, just screwed himself up into a ball and made noises like a cow. I sat and watched, waiting for it to end. 'Wet twat,' Darren muttered, before leaving us alone.

Jon only had enough time to cry through one rushed cycle of stiff, blunt sobs before the whistle went and the commentary began again, and the room filled up with young, heavy male breasts and blood sugar. For the rest of the game, he didn't look away from the screen once. When it was over . . . In fact, I do not know what we did after that. I only remember his red face, and his mussed hair, and the sickening wish that I had the strength or the courage to break one of those bottles and use it to open up his brother's cheek.

'I'll get to the shops then,' I tell Jon.

'Thanks man.'

'Then I'll see about gazebos.'

'Ta.'

I collect my own slim black briefcase, and leave the music shop.

THERE ARE SHADOWBEASTS AT THE PARTY. THEY ARE GRAZING.

The party has been going for about an hour. There is a banner in the living room declaring Jon's mum's fiftieth birthday, which seems wrong. This milestone must have been, as I have said (if I have said anything here) at least a decade ago. Could be two decades ago. Maybe it's a joke and they've been getting this same banner out for years. But maybe not?

It occurs to me that Jon will have expected me to change it somehow, or gone to get a new one. If Jon mentions it, I'll just say I didn't have time. I try and calm down about the banner, but find that I am shaking, my breath is weird. I have been rushing around a lot, so maybe just low blood sugar. I take long breaths. I say 'raisin face' with a scrunched-up face, then 'pumpkin face' with a big wide face. 'This is a face exercise,' I say to myself. I do it three times and slowly the shaking stops. Since nobody else has mentioned this mistake, I decide, I am completely permitted to just not say anything.

Jon's brother is on the sofa, taking up space, along with a couple of those friends I remember. They have names like Fin and Hutch and Pete Brown. They are the same basic models as they used to be, but older, balder and tempered by the respectability of their jobs. Fin works in IT and has eczema. Hutch is a plumber, hoping his fourteen-year-old son will join the business one day. Pete Brown is signed off with stress from his job in a local primary school. They are watching the match.

When I arrived, I politely said hello and, since they didn't react, I added, 'Ah the footy!'

I got nothing back from that either. They just stared at the television. I thought, peripherally, that I saw Jon's brother exchange a look with the one called Hutch, but I can't be sure. When I looked directly at them, they were fixated again by the television.

I tried looking at the game. I didn't recognise the teams, one in red, one in blue. Each player carrying their slim black briefcase in their hand with a straight arm. Most of the players carried the brief-case in their right hand, but a few carried them in their left.

I made the mistake of pointing out how graceful it was, how they moved with their briefcases. How they could come so close to touching, but then swerve away. None of the men responded. The silence became heavy.

I made an excuse to get away to the kitchen, where I have been for the last forty-five minutes. Outside, in the communal gardens down below, the party is well under way. They are waiting for my guacamole.

My briefcase is in the corner, under one of the two chairs that are tucked in either side of the small breakfast table. I don't remember carrying it here. I remember trying to leave it in the supermarket – thinking it would be fine to just walk away from it, so I left it on the floor beside the till. I stare at the shimmering leather, reflecting my leg. Reflecting the rest of the kitchen, but not faithfully, just areas of light.

I believe it was handed back to me as I left the supermarket by the security guard. He wordlessly handed it over.

No, wait.

He did not hand it over, because he wouldn't have touched it. He stopped me leaving the shop, and gently, but meaningfully, as though he'd had to do it a thousand times already that day, stood in my way and gestured for me to go back and get the briefcase. If I close my eyes I see his face, scraped raw from shaving, the security guard. Sending me back for my briefcase with an air of exasper-ation at the state of the world.

I look out of the window. Many animals have come with the guests to the party. They graze in the areas away from the gaze-bos and barbecues, in the wilder parts of the communal area. As I watch and mash avocados, one of the guests turns up to look at me. She is holding her briefcase. It does not match her pale floral chemise, and yet looks natural. She is waving at me.

'Come on down! We're all waiting for you!'

I hold up the salad bowl full of guacamole and show her. There is a lot of guacamole now. I've used seventeen avocados.

'Nearly done!' I shout. I tilt the bowl at a very risky angle, to show her the amount of guacamole I have made.

'Oh,' she says. 'That's a big bowlful, isn't it? Is that a normal amount for people then?'

A few people around her laugh at this. A man emerges from one of the loose circles of other men and puts his arm around her waist. He is stroking her bum when he calls up.

'You been sick, have you?' He oinks out a laugh at his own question.

'No, it's guacamole,' I shout back.

He isn't listening. He's leading the woman away. His hand is spread across the small of her back.

'I'll be down in a minute then,' I shout.

'Can't wait,' says the man, without looking back.

I am distracted by a sound erupting from the living room. Someone has scored a goal.

Darren comes in, it's impossible to judge from his face who has scored, if the news is good or bad for his team.

'Hi Darren,' I say. He ignores me, opens the fridge and looks inside. He's wearing a burgundy shirt that's much too tight for him. He must have bought it fifteen years ago. Between the buttons,

I can see his white skin and dark body hair. His navy chinos are equally snug.

'Getting a beer?' I ask.

'You want one?' he asks. For a moment, I seem to make sense to Darren, now that I want beer. I'm overwhelmed.

'Yes please, Darren. If there's enough.'

He wordlessly hands me a huge can of Stella Artois and watches me holding it. I stand there with my can of Stella Artois. It's like holding a cold white shell casing. I do not like this drink, though I do like the rhyming slang for it, which Darren uses. He calls it a 'Nelson', for Nelson Mandela – Stella.

'Is your mum around?' I ask.

'Down there,' he points down the hallway to a yellowing door that is smaller than the others.

'She's still in her room?'

Darren shrugs.

'Would she mind if I go knock?'

'Do what you fucking like, mate,' says Darren, and then he clumps back into the living room.

I hear him muttering, 'Don't ask about me, will you? "How's it going Darren?" "Oh, fine thanks, yeah, it's been a while." Just have some of my beer and don't say thank you, fuckssake twat . . .'

Alone now, but still concerned Darren will notice if I just return it to the fridge, I open the can and take a long drink. It is so cold it freezes my head for a moment.

I stand alone and drink more of the lager. It feels like I have swallowed a lot of it, but the can remains intimidatingly heavy in my hand.

THE SOUND OF SHRINKING FILLS THE AIR.

In the corridor I see Pete Brown, he's on his mobile phone, whispering and hunching his shoulders.

'I don't know,' he is saying, 'I can't be sure at all. Why would you ask me that?' All the vowels are hissed out as he speaks.

'Uh, Pete,' I say. He looks at me with a sort of sneer on his face, then with worry.

'I'm sorry man, I don't mean to interrupt. I'm looking for Jon's mum.'

Pete Brown points down the corridor. 'Seventh door on the right,' he says.

The other doors are narrow and dirty. I don't remember there being so many. They don't have handles, but Yale locks, like front doors, or the janitor's cupboard at school. The fifth one is hanging open.

I turn back to thank Pete Brown, but he is some distance away from me now, vanishing round the corner into the kitchen.

The walls of Jon's mother's bedroom are pleated and pulling in. It's like being inside a raisin. I find Jon's mother in there, sitting on her bed. All around her are clothes and piles of books. It seems like they have all been moved away from the sagging walls. The piles are neat but exasperated. The ceiling sags like cloth.

Jon's mother's face lights up when I come in, the same as it always has, as if she wants nothing but happiness for you. But of course, she cannot do anything about it, so you never ask her for anything, you just live in the smile and the feeling of how happy, just how happy she wants you to be.

'Won't you come to the party?' I ask. 'Everyone's here.'

The smile fades a little, but she is glad there is a party, somehow this is clear. Her voice is shockingly clear when she speaks, like a song.

'No – I really didn't want a fuss this year. I'm awfully tired, to be honest.'

The walls darken. 'You shouldn't stay in here though,' I say. 'It can't be good for your health.'

'Oh, I'm all right.' She hunches up a little more away from the walls.

'Please,' I say. 'It's been so long since I saw you, and I have made you my guacamole.'

'Oh, well, I do like your guacamole. Have you made tortilla chips?'

'There's lots of those.'

'Oh well, then maybe. Maybe.'

'I'll tell you what, maybe we could go together? I don't know many people. I'm afraid of them, actually.'

'You're afraid of them?' She laughs at this. 'How funny to hear that you are afraid of things. Do you remember, you used to go around in that plastic top. You used to wear those pink sunglasses and never cared what they said about you.'

The walls now were fully brown and there was a creaking sound. The air was damp and smelling rotten.

'I think we have to get out of this room.'

'The landlord. It's the landlord, he won't listen.'

She gestures around the collapsing raisin walls.

'We'll talk to him,' I say. I reach out for her hand. It's warm and dry. I can feel her individual finger bones rolling under the skin. She seems pained by it. I let go.

'How's your mum?' she asks. I check her smile for signs she is covering up any pain. I really hadn't held her hand that tightly at all.

'Uh, she's fine, you know,' I say. 'Same as always.'

'I see her on Saturdays,' Jon's mother tells me. 'She's gardening now, isn't she? She does the flower displays in Talisman Square.'

I don't remember the flowers in Talisman Square. It's a shopping area, low-rise fronts with concrete awnings. There are benches in the centre of the square. I picture my mother in a large hat, as I last saw her, in a pale lavender vest that bunches on her thin, sunned shoulders. When I last saw her, she was crouching, shaking with the effort of this pose. She asked me to fetch something and I went out for it. I do not remember if I returned.

'Shall we go outside, hey?' I ask Jon's mother.

'Is it all ready? I've been pretending not to notice for hours and hours. I think they forgot to come and get me.'

She is tiny and white. The walls of the room seem to be tugging her further in. She seems hard to reach, and I have to walk forward several steps and reach out my hand to pull her up. She is unsteady rising. It costs her dearly to get to the door. She seems tired and does not answer when I ask, repeatedly, if she is all right. Her sleek black briefcase hangs in her left hand by her side.

AN ELECTRICAL EVENT HAS DESTROYED THE IGNITION OF MANY PARKED CARS

We are outside on the grass. Jon's mum has her arm through mine. When we see Jon walking towards us across the communal gardens, she ticks him off for wearing his work clothes to the party, but she is smiling the whole time.

'Look at the gazebos, Jon!' she says. 'Thank you love. Thank you so much.'

She leaves me and goes off with him. I find the gazebo where the drinks are. I realise I have left my Stella Artois upstairs. Darren won't be happy about that at all. I left quite a lot in the can.

I put my briefcase down and pour myself a warm Pimm's and sugar-free lemonade. I can't face adding the strawberries and cucumber. It looks like a pint of cola. It tastes of liquified ants.

There's a commotion in one of the other gazebos. I only erected two, but now I can see seven or eight of them dotted across the vast green space between the tall pale-brick residential blocks.

I head towards the commotion. Some of the guests seem to be shoving each other. Men in tight knee-length denim shorts with dyed blond hair and red faces. I try to see if Jon is there, but as I arrive I don't recognise any of the people. I realise it could be another party. It could be for anyone.

I send Jon a message on my phone.

Hey buddy, I am a bit lost. I've wandered into a different party, I think.

There's no reply. By the time I get back to the original party, there's nobody there except a cousin of Jon's I met once at his sister's wedding.

'Where is everyone?' I ask him. He wipes his non-briefcase hand on his jeans. It leaves an ugly black stain.

'No idea my friend,' he says. 'Nobody here but us chickens!'

I make a laughing sound, but it's not at all funny what he just said.

'Can you help me with my car?' he asks. 'I need a push.'

I look around at the debris from the party. One of the gazebos has fallen over. A couple of the others have collapsed together like dinosaurs with their skin flapping in the wind.

The thought of clearing it all up on my own fills me with rage.

'Sure,' I say. 'I can help you.'

I follow him across the grass. There is no shade. My hands are sweaty. I let go of my briefcase and leave it on the ground. I walk for a long time before I realise that the man I was following has gone, and there is nothing but this communal green area and, at the end of it, a low dark railing.

square / recess / moon

Can you see those towers down there, on the other side of the city? That's where he was living at the time. In one of those tangled-together buildings. I can't tell you which one, but he was definitely high up in the towers there. I know because he talked about it a lot. Also, I live around there too. Different tower, but I know the general area.

Ah, OK, I see you have an address, so I'm guessing you already tried to go there. Let me see? Yeah, that's what I thought – you have a street number, but that's just the building. I'm sorry. If you don't have the exact apartment, it is impossible. You should give up now, that's my advice.

Listen; they cross over inside, those places. The textile workers who built that tower hundreds of years ago, they built it like a small town in there. All the apartments have connections to other apartments so families have direct pathways to one another. I'm not talking about connecting dwellings that have just a door between them. I mean families on different floors, in different parts of the building – in fact in any one of the other dozens of towers – were able to find each other. It was for safety, you understand, and for the young. A complete nursery network through the hearts of several buildings.

Connections that mean nothing to us now, obviously, and that don't make any sense at all. You can get lost in there, and never find your way out, you know what I mean? If I were you, I'd leave it well alone. Nice meeting you.

Oh, you're following me. Well, I can see you don't want to give up. This is someone you cared about? Well, OK, here – I'm hungry. And I'll take that envelope with cash that you keep touching when you put your hand in your pocket. Let's go in here – this is a good place to sit and talk and eat food. You're paying of course.

In every apartment, there is a sort of living space that nobody uses. You don't use it, there's no light. You dump your stuff there if you have any stuff, and that's it. Sometimes, if you've lost your keys or a jacket, it might be in that dark room, but generally you stay out of it. There's a sort of feeling in that room that is not nice. A historical feeling, one with its connection broken. Does that make sense? Not much of it will. There is a bedroom, which is a place for being unconscious in and nothing else. And then in every apartment, without exception, there is a good, warming kitchen. He liked the kitchen.

'Sometimes,' he said to me once, 'I find it hard to get out of the kitchen. Or, not the kitchen, but the dining area of the kitchen.'

This was about a month before he stopped turning up at work.

We were out for lunch when he told me about the dining area in his kitchen. It was my idea to go out for lunch in a bar – he wasn't the type to instigate it – though he said yes quickly enough. There was something automatic about the way he agreed to things, you know? As though coming for lunch with us was something he had been craving, and yet could not articulate or arrange for it himself. The words *Can I join you for lunch?* somehow felt impossible to him, or so it seemed.

Some people are like that – but they get by. They are among us all the time, these nervous people. Nobody knows why they came here, where it's hard to get on with people, where the buildings are mazes. The sun, you see that? Who would come here?

He arrived in town alone, that tells me something – at some point he *decided* to come here. He had enough propulsion to pack a bag, and to set off. He had it in him to choose.

Sorry, perhaps the idea of him packing and leaving – perhaps this is painful to you? Or maybe more time has passed than I thought. Perhaps this was all before you were born? It feels like only yesterday.

Sorry, I must stop for a moment.

Sorry for that pause – I think about him a lot, but it's hard to imagine him choosing things, taking control. I try to picture his face as he makes a decision, but I can't. I'm sorry. This is not why you came.

Excuse me. As I was saying, I wanted a long lunch. I needed to get out of the office, if you want the truth. The place was dying around us. I was badly in need of a distraction from the work I was failing to do. Our friend always seemed to be up to date with his projects. He could always make time for extra meetings and so on so I dragged him out with me. He was unaffected by the obvious calamity of our company's situation. He turned up, smiled at the right time, did his work, let it all wash over him. He was a lifeboat in a sea of dead boats – that's how I saw him then anyway. Does that make sense?

I'll continue. We were day-drinking, as I have said. The company we worked for was not progressing well. We were circling the drain, and even though there was financing, there was nothing going on in the sales team. It was a depressing situation, but it didn't affect him. Not at all. I think he planned to just work there, do his level best, until the place went under. Then I imagine he would have expected to find somewhere else he could quietly sit and carefully, efficiently re-evaluate the technology stack of a new company that was wasting money and couldn't understand why. There is a lot of work in this town. A lot of work and not much else. Well, towers, obviously. Plenty of towers.

Anyway, that lunchtime we went to the bar across the square from the office. I didn't tell him this, but I planned to drink the whole afternoon. I needed company.

The place was called Gerrards. It was one of those bars that crop up within the ground floor of large office buildings. You enter through a heavy smoked-glass door into an open space, walled with more smoked glass. The bar staff are interchangeable with the reception staff in the business entrance on the other side of the building. The toilets for the bar are actually the guest toilets for the meeting rooms on the first floor and basement.

We sat on a sofa eating chips. I tried to move things along, but he just wanted bottles of beer, slow-drinking, to his credit – he didn't mind that I was doubling his pace. He didn't mind.

He was silent. No choice really, trying to look interested while I held forth about how I was going to get sacked or the company was going to go under and I didn't know which was coming first. After a while I became sick of hearing myself talk, so I asked him about himself, how he was finding things. I was on the verge of begging him to talk to me about anything, anything at all, just to keep me from whining. And that was how he started talking about that room of his. The dining area of the kitchen.

'I can't stop thinking about it,' he said. 'I think about being in that room all the time. Like, I never really leave. Or I do, but somehow I don't.'

I found this a very odd thing to say, of course, but I told him, 'That's normal. That's totally normal. You're in a new town. You need something to anchor you. It's totally normal to like a room.'

'Yes. I suppose that's true,' he said, but he didn't seem satisfied. Then he said, 'I keep a little verbena plant on a shelf, just below the window. There's a table with two chairs, one of which I think of as the main chair, it faces straight out of the window, across the table. That's my chair.'

'So if I ever come over I'll sit on the other chair then, will I?'

He didn't really hear me. He went on describing the room. He moved his hands to where the various features of this room were in relation to where we were sitting. He closed his eyes on certain words, nodding as if to confirm to himself, yes this is *window*. Yes, here is *chair*. I found myself relaxing into the idea of this room.

'The curtains are a kind of rust-red,' he told me. 'Linen they are, thin enough to blow in the breeze, and to let the moon glow through – where the weave is thicker, the material fractures the light ever so gently. The walls are the colour of butter, or yellowed ivory, and made of this bulky, soft mortar.' He stroked his cheek as he talked about the walls, and I realised he was imagining it against his skin. 'I can't describe what it's made of, the wall plastering, I don't have the words, but it is like art. It's like a sculpture in plaster, everything is smooth and organic like a softened cave.'

At this point I was just nodding along. It's odd, isn't it? But I was no longer embarrassed. I should have been, because who talks like this? But you have to understand, I could see that room – there is the window, the sky beyond it, the tiles on the roofs outside like the rippling tides of a sea. There is the cold plaster, butter-yellow. I can close my eyes and see it all now, just as I describe it to you.

'It's so nice,' I told him. Even through the booze, I was deadly serious, this room now sounded like heaven to me.

'The walls have these recesses which form incidental shelves. I have a lamp in one of these. In the evenings, I put the lamp on and it glows in the little recess – it looks like a sentry there, chubby in the recess. The night air comes in and mixes the fragrance of the city with the soft citrus of the verbena plant.'

I had my eyes closed by now. I felt myself there completely as he told me about the floor tiles, how cool they were. He told me again, but in a new way, about how the light hit the roofs that lay below the window and all around. The tiles like a sea.

We came to a natural break in the description of the room, and then it was just us again, sitting together in this weird numbness. I slapped my legs, got him another beer.

After that, we spoke regularly, but we didn't go out together again. Whenever we found ourselves alone together, I made sure the emphasis of the chat was firmly back on the shit state of things in the company – which is to say, I did all the talking. He would drop something in from time to time. He got into the habit of telling me about the book he was reading, which in fact he had been struggling with since he'd found it in his apartment when he moved here.

It was about a couple of fictional mountaineers, this book. They were climbing a deadly, unscalable mountain. I think the idea was that somehow this mountain was bigger than Everest, and it had come in the night, or something. A sudden, weird mountain. Very far-fetched, very pointless. Anyway, this vast thing that dwarfed the mighty Everest was being climbed by two mountaineers, but get this – the whole book wasn't even about how this fictional mountain came to be there. It was instead about the toxic relationship between these two climbers. This intensely damaged relationship the climbers had with each other was the focus of the whole story. At one point – I think this is right – several hundred bats the size of men emerged from a cave and beset them, tearing at their flesh, but the scene was forgotten after barely half a page, the bats having been easy to kill with crampons and ice hacks. After that, he told me, for a hundred more pages they were just teasing each other, and claiming petty victories of spite – insulting each other's table manners, being offensive about the smell they had, or one of them claiming to have swindled money from the other's parents. Always bringing each other down emotionally, working tirelessly to harm the confidence of the other mountaineer, so progress was painfully slow. For the sake of winning these increasingly petty quarrels, they risked losing limbs, even death. A load of shit.

He told me it was agony to read it, but he was determined to get to the end. 'Like being a mountaineer yourself,' I joked.

'Yes!' he agreed. 'Exactly, I think that might be the point of the book.'

Anyway, I was fine hearing about it, but then he told me how he read it mostly at home, in a large recess in the wall of the dining area of his kitchen. As soon as he told me about sitting there, with this dreary book, I could see it, the little recess just big enough for him to fit in there, the smooth plaster on the walls, the leaves of the verbena rustling softly. I could see the light, soft as cream, blending from the moon to the little lamp in its own recess, to the gentle burn of the gas hob. I felt as though I was there with him. I felt that embarrassment again, followed by a wave of sudden weariness.

I had to slap myself in the legs again to snap out of it. Then he let me rage on about the state of the company, the woolliness of the CEO, how I had lost all confidence in the place, how things were falling apart around us and we didn't have any way of stopping it – I was boring myself to be honest. We parted ways at the end of that particular day and from then on I stayed away from him – not wanting to bring him down, that's what I told myself, but also I began to find it harder and harder to be around him. Whenever he spoke, he would mention his room. And I felt hypnotised, found myself enveloped there with him, embarrassed and fatigued.

I few weeks later, I found him in a state of quite serious distress – he was late to the office, something that almost never happened. I assumed he was just sick or feeling tired. I had been feeling bad for neglecting him. Taking some of those assholes from the QA team out for drinks instead of inviting him. He hadn't said anything, but he kept meeting my eye, and I would smile and find excuses to be somewhere else. Awful of me, I'm sorry.

I found him in the breakout room. He was sitting at the white table staring straight ahead into space. He looked a wreck, I'm sorry to say. His hair was out of shape. He had a smell coming off him. I didn't realise he'd noticed I was even there until he began speaking.

'I felt myself fading away,' he said. 'I don't know what's happening to me.'

'What do you mean fading away? Like passing out?'

'No. Not passing out. I was in a queue, and after a while I realised I had been waiting so long, I couldn't remember what the queue was for. I was just standing there behind this tall man, somehow I couldn't manoeuvre myself out of the line to see what was at the other end. The tall man kept moving too. Nobody would move out of my way.'

'Jeez, we've all been there,' I said. 'I *fade away*, as you call it, all the time in queues. You're probably just tired. Head home maybe?'

'No, it wasn't like that. I literally didn't know the time of day. It could have been a lunch place or a coffee truck. The queue went round the corner of the building – I had no idea what was going on. And then I could smell verbena. I could hear the curtains flapping in the breeze.'

'Eh?'

'I could feel the tiles beneath me, I could feel the sun gradually moving across the table. I could see the little lamp like a man in the recess. I saw the sun move, and the leaves of the verbena grew. I was there for hours. I cleaned the table, I touched the walls . . .'

'I think we need to get outside somewhere,' I told him.

I took him under the arm and hurried him out of the breakout room towards the exit, and into a lift.

I couldn't explain to him at the time, but as he was speaking, I myself lost focus. I found myself in his room – the dining area of his kitchen – or not actually in the room, but I felt the sense of the room. My friend's sad eyes had turned away from me as he spoke, and for an instant, I couldn't see him at all. The room was there instead.

Outside in the square, the city noise and the cool air cleared my head slightly.

'Are you all right?' I asked. 'You feeling better out here?'

'Better,' he said.

He did not look better at all. He looked panicked. I wanted to leave him there. His window and the verbena plant flickered as he stood there. I wanted to run away and never speak to him again, but I could not. It wasn't his fault, whatever was going on.

I put my arm through his, and we walked through the square and off towards the South City Road. After some time, as we dodged around the mid-morning crowd, he spoke again.

'You're the only person I speak to in this town. I don't speak to a single other living soul.' We were essentially lost in the streets when he said this. I was trying to get a grip, but I dared not look at him in case he was a curtain.

'That's no good!' I said. 'No friends? We'll have to fix that! You always look so happy in the office. Or at least contented. I assumed you had people!' I was lying, it was clear that he had no people. I felt dreadful.

'You gave me a bit of a scare,' I said, after he seemed to have calmed down.

'I'm better now,' he said.

'Are you sure?'

'Yes, I want to go home.'

I walked him home and we didn't say anything else. I didn't look at him, not even to say goodbye as he slipped through his doorway in the white base of the towers.

The next day he was mugged outside on the street. I don't know exactly what happened – he told me about it, but he couldn't give me the full details. Someone rushed him from behind, shoved him to the ground, took his bag, took his wallet. Left his phone. He didn't say anything else about it – not the exact location, no description of the mugger, nothing.

I know that he had several important documents taken from him. Precious objects, he called them, Documents and pictures.

'They didn't see me at all,' he said. He was talking about being at the police station, where they don't stand on politeness the way I might. He tried to report the crime, but they didn't see him. They saw a window. Do you understand? He was talking but they saw roof tiles, they saw a pleasant sky.

He was saying pictures of my daughter. He was saying my life has been stolen, but they saw plaster and they smelt verbena.

Eventually he had to leave the police station. He tried making a phone call but dry green leaves curled at the edges instead. The curtains blew in the wind.

I spoke to him that night. He contacted me through the work messaging system, which I stupidly have on my phone. I agreed to meet up.

He said he wanted to have dinner so we went to a Chinese place near the towers. Good food. Cheap.

He was all right eating. We talked about dumb stuff. Some work gossip. He said he felt bad for Ollie, a young guy who had recently joined. He worked late every day, but nobody would promote him because there was no money.

'Why doesn't he get it?' he said. 'Silly idiot!'

It was the first serious work conversation I had ever had with him.

'Don't you want to talk about the police?' I asked. 'You were mugged. What happened?'

But he didn't want to talk about it. Instead, we talked about the bookshop in town, what they had in the window there. We talked about the fountains in the park.

For a while the cold moon shone through and cast the wooden table in a broad paleness. The verbena shivered in the cold. I had to go to the bathroom and wash my face.

It seemed that when he was eating, he held up OK.

'I still don't know anything about you really,' I said to him. 'What do you like doing?'

He started talking, but instead of him, there was the window. There was the table and the best chair facing the window. There was the lamp. Over to my right was the hob. He was saying something but there were clouds processing over the distant chimneys, the creak of a beetle investigating the soil of the plant pot. I watched for a long time as the moon in the dining area of his kitchen completely replaced his face.

When he finally spoke again, he said, 'I like swimming. I love to swim but I haven't seen anywhere in this town that suits me.'

Determined not to see the room again, I asked him if he'd tried the Sorrel Centre.

'I've tried. But too many people. Too much of a crowd.'

'What about over in South Point?'

'I went there, but the place was closed. It looked good though. Quiet.'

We agreed to go down to South Point for a swim soon. I felt weird agreeing to this. He sensed my hesitation, I think, because he said, 'Look, I'll be there at six a.m. tomorrow. If you can't make it, don't worry. But I'll be there. I need to at least have the appointment – it will motivate me,' he said.

'Really? Six a.m. tomorrow?'

'Six a.m.! Oh yeah!'

He tried to make it sound like a joke, but I could hear a snag in his voice, like he was actually quite nervous about what would happen to him in a swimming pool. Would someone drown as they swam out towards the blue sky above the rooftops?

'Six a.m.!' I said. 'I'll be there.'

'It'll be great!' He was actually smiling.

'I can't promise to match your sunny mood!'

'Haha!'

'Haha!'

We stayed for drinks at the Chinese place, which was a mistake because I lost concentration and for a long time the curtains billowed, the rust-red curtains, the verbena plant on the shelf under the window hushed as cool air and the night fragrance of the city came in, clouds pushed shadows across the butter-yellow walls, the lamp squatted like a little man in the silver light, guarding his recess in the wall. I felt the sudden sensation that I was falling, plummeting into ice, because in the room was a figure, a hand wiping dust from the table – a terrible horrible sadness came over me.

'Six a.m.!' my friend said again. The sadness lifted instantly. His face, his cheery face saying a stupid time of the morning, was back.

I never made it to the swimming pool. I haven't seen him since that night in the Chinese restaurant, but I'm telling you, he's in that room. That's what I'm saying, it makes no difference, I have no idea where exactly his room is. It's a maze in there, you could try all week and never find it. Even if you have the address, the address is no good, I told you that. The whole place crosses over and repeats, like a ritual. And in every apartment, in every space, a room so tranquil, so utterly harmonious that if you're not careful it will replace you.

But you already know that because right now I see the sun going down through a window, a chair turning grey in silhouette. I am talking to you but the curtain is flapping in the breeze, the plaster is butter-yellow.

You are listening but there is now just a window. You are listening but there is only a table set in front of the window, a bat flickers past changing direction, rippling the air. The roof tiles shrink in the cold.

A window, a table, a recess with a lamp.

A window and the grey light, a table.

A moon looking in.

The figure is there. The figure, starved and tall, grumbles by the table, shuffling, wrapped tightly in material. The figure moves slowly, casting the shadows of ribbons fluttering in the sea air, devouring the light into its mouth, dusting the table, cooking beans. The figure there all day, running long, obsessive hands over the verbena plant – hours go by, days go by, the figure, the window the ocean of the tiles on the roofs that scale the lost and most forlorn night.

The people in the kitchen

I spoke to the people in the kitchen just now. They seemed fine with the idea – which is typical of this company of people, they breeze along easily with everything I say.

Resurrect me from the dead! At midnight!

Sure, fine, no worries, buddy.

We were in a horseshoe shape. I had their full attention.

I have taken the dose, I said. I now place myself in your hands. You will all have to act, if I am to be brought back to life.

I let it sink in, and gave them time for questions.

Nobody asked me any questions.

The people in the kitchen were like fish, I thought. Very beautiful fish, each scaled in lovely knitwear, and facially they were deco-rated, invisibly, with protective patterns and symbols.

My father lives in this town, I was saying to one of them earlier. He's an assistant in a local solicitor's, my father. Worked there for years. In winter, he's in knits. In summer, in shirts. In spring, it's tank tops and short sleeves. In autumn I don't know.

Michael – that was the name of the man I was talking to – he asked me whereabouts the solicitor's was. He knew several of the local firms, he said, because he was a rep for a drinking water company. He did all the small offices. All over town.

I asked Michael to remind me of the name of the town we were in.

Ah no – I realised. No no no. It was another town he worked in. Far away. My father is far away. I have no connections to this place.

Also, my father is a teacher. Far away, a teacher of some kind.

Michael changed the subject. How did I come to be here, at this party?

I was invited on a whim, I told him. I was specifically invited because people had heard about my party trick.

Yes, but who? asked Michael.

I'm sorry, Michael, I said after a while. I can't help you there.

The people who invited me to the party are strangers. They are no longer here. I saw them leaving, long before I went into the kitchen. I happened to be looking out of the window, and they emerged from the house down below and – actually I can't exactly recall what happened to them next. There was a sound, like violins.

It's *Flatliners*! I explained to the people in the horseshoe in the kitchen.

The film, *Flatliners*. Just like Kiefer Sutherland and his student friends. It's when you die and come back super powerful because your soul has left your body, and it has been replaced by a demon.

Except I have learnt how to stay close to my body, so I can come back in when you resurrect me.

I will have some of the powers of a demon but still I will be my own self.

What kind of powers? someone asked. Michael, probably, that guy!

Simple powers, I said, as casually as I could. Common demon powers. I would more precisely describe them as skills, really.

Like what? asked Michael. He was drinking a very arrogant drink at the time.

Michael, I said. Have you ever seen demon calligraphy?

No, he said.

Well, get ready!

Before he could waste any more of my time, I repeated my instructions to the group.

I have taken the dose, I said. I really am relying on you all.

They continued smoking and having a nice time, but they seemed fine with how serious this all was in terms of their responsibility.

I handed the written instructions to Jason, who was closest to me in the horseshoe. We had known each other for perhaps as long as two hours.

Jason was the one I trusted the most at this party. He kept touching me on the shoulder, or maybe holding himself up.

Yes, it's possible I was actually a kind of support for him. He kept leaning on me, I remember now, and saying:

'I don't think that's what that movie was about, man.'

But that's typical of Jason – he is absolutely on another planet. But I have convinced him, I think, that I will be dead and he must act.

But will he act?

I am alone now, I am waiting for Jason and the others.

I'm trying to remember what the town is called, and what the party is for.

On the train here – I came through a long passage of sea mist. We were in the mist for a long time. There were several occasions when I felt the brushing of a membrane against my fingertips. The fine softness of a baby's head. The webbing between the fingers of a bat.

These sensations were obviously manifestations of something else. Obviously Jason. Was Jason the right choice?

Nevermind, it's too late to worry about Jason – once you've taken the dose, things get pretty carefree – this is all part of it.

It is essential to be relaxed about what's coming.

But then it also means you can be somewhat laissez-faire about details. Like, can they even read my handwriting?

I feel ashamed too, every time I do this, I feel ashamed. I think, I should be at home. I should not have left my desk suddenly this afternoon and gone to the train station.

I remember breaking a tooth.

I'm lying in the bedroom now, in the attic of the party house, where I will temporarily leave my body for a while.

I do not know whose bedroom this is. It looks like Sylvia's room. It can't actually be Sylvia's room. Sylvia lives far away, and anyway has a different room now.

Sylvia's room did not have a guitar. Sylvia's room did not have a living plant in it. Sylvia's room had cups in it, and a large pillow, and a tin where she kept tobacco and rolling papers. Sylvia's room had a single bed, and a sloped ceiling.

I do not know this room. I have sent the text message to Jason.

Jason, I am in the attic. Time is approaching. Soon I will need to be resurrected.

Sure man, coming right up.

That's what Jason's reply said.

I can't do anything about it now, anyway. I can feel a red blanket coming over me, and this is part of the soul separating itself from the body.

I think I can feel it, the red blanket. In my mouth I can taste olives. This too is part of the process.

Also, I have eaten some olives.

I go to sleep.

I am not asleep any more.

They are here.

Of course, by now I realise that the effects of the mixture have not been strong enough and I'm not dead at all when Jason comes into the bedroom.

Jason is in the presence of four or five beasts – or party guests – they gather around the bed.

I am here, he says.

Then, to the others: He's dead! Fuck. Actually, what the fuck.

They repeat amongst themselves: He's dead. Oh shit, they say. He's dead. They don't even touch my body. He's totally beige, one of them says.

He's the colour of death. He's the colour of wet pages. He's gone his eyes are completely dead.

As I have indicated, this is not the case. I'm not even medically unwell. And yet they go on.

He's the colour of slush on the road.

I'm quite well.

Do the thing, Jason, one of them says. It could be Michael. He's the type who would start giving out orders.

You have to do it now. Bring him back or he'll be dead forever.

But I'm not dead. I'm just really very accepting. I've accepted something fundamental that they cannot see. Someone is calling an ambulance, but this is quite unnecessary.

Finally, shakingly, Jason begins to perform the ritual. He and the others who I can see clearly now are not beasts but ordinary party guests.

Jason reads from the instructions I gave him.

The instructions that are to bring me back to life. He begins with the standard opening words that I have carefully written.

Oh biscuit! he cries.

He does a really excellent loud voice. But the words are not as I wrote them.

Oh hardened skinless brain!

One of the other party guests starts repeating what Jason says, echoing it in a hushed voice like a mystical poet.

Oh dry seed.

(Oh dry seed.)

Bless you for this, I tell the echo party guest. Thank you so much, I say. Although not with words.

I speak no words to Jason or anyone else. Not even to explain that these things they're saying are not the true incantation to bring an absent soul back to its body. Jason is freelancing. He is making it all up.

It is lucky I am not really dead.

Although I'm not dead, I have reached a state of such acceptance that I cannot speak.

I cannot speak or do anything that would cause friction in the passing of things. An eyelash would be an unforgivable outrage.

An eyelash would snag the stillness like a great sail. A grain of skin'd drag like a stone face.

I am not breathing at all, of course. Nor is my heart beating. But I am quite alive.

I am as accepting as a lake of pure stone.

Jason considers the words on the page. Then 'reads' on:

Oh confection! Oh orange juice!

(Oh orange juice.)

Wad!

(Wad.)

Sylvia comes into the room. She stands behind Jason. Hello Sylvia, I say (again not with words).

She asks them to leave her room. Jason continues the ritual. He screeches rapidly:

Highlighter pens are my favourite kind of pen! And yet I never use them correctly!

Jason is not reading the correct incantation. What is this rubbish about highlighter pens? Sylvia is asking them to leave. Several go.

But Jason remains where he is. He says he must resurrect me, but as we know I am alive.

Even though it's embarrassing to rise up from the bed as Jason says:

I always lose the caps!

I do rise up. I tell Sylvia how it's good to see her, and I like what she's done with the place, then I swim in darkness.

I swim in darkness to the kitchen.

I swim in darkness to the lake.

I swim in darkness to the car park and see children as young as twelve throwing stolen cans of deodorant into a flaming bin.

I swim in darkness to the swimming pool. I touch the blue gilded water with my extended hand.

I call it a hand but a better word would be sensing outpost. It's not a hand for holding things.

I could not hold anything I can only accept things.

I accept in darkness to the swimming pool. I accept myself into the vending machine.

Oh savoury! I imagine Jason saying.

Jason is still at the party. He has been tasked with cooking a lasagne from frozen. Everyone is counting on him.

I don't have to see him to know that he has no idea where the oven is or how it works.

I don't have to have real hands to sense the pain in his fingers from standing there for too long holding the frozen lasagne.

I don't have to sense anything.

You and me, and Russel Palomet

It's a June day, and I've packed my suitcase. Off I go!

I'm out the door and on the road where I live. It's a fine wide road, and my house is a long way behind me now. I'm worrying calmly about the gas and the bath. About the TV, and the kettle, and the leaking paint. Less calmly about the paint. The paint has been leaking from the top of its tin for well over a year, a drip at a time. Down it goes, into the crack, and in the crack there is only darkness. I've tried to see where the paint might be pooling in the crack, or coming out from the other side of the wood with the crack, but it doesn't come out.

I've packed my suitcase, and I have now left the road on which I live. I'm coming to see you. I love you. I am excited because we have agreed to go on holiday and we have spent all our money on the tickets. I've not eaten a proper meal this week so I could afford to enjoy the holiday to the absolute maximum. I think the paint is probably just being absorbed into the wood somehow, in between the grain. I want our holiday to be the greatest experience you have ever had.

I have not asked you what your current greatest-ever experience is, because it might be something that cannot be topped. You might have been skiing, and been really good at skiing and extremely popular with everyone in the ski lodge. You might have dived from a plane. You might have had a near-death encounter and been brought back to life and seen the colours all around you as though for the first time – the absolute beauty of the world –

and felt more alive than you ever did before. I haven't asked, so I don't know. I hope you have a great time on our holiday anyway. I'm sure the gas is off. I'm sure I've packed everything. In my mind, I can see my passport in the bag. Foreign travel makes me so tired, but I'm not used to it, so that might be why. I can't wait to get to your house. I think we will have time for a cup of tea before we go. I'm going to ask if you have plasters. I'm going to run through a whole list of things I think we might need.

I'm ready for you to dispel many of these ideas as overkill or just too complicated to get hold of now. I think that's fine. I'm looking forward to the trip to the airport on the train. That will be great because we might buy a coffee and a sandwich – just one of each and we will share them. And possibly some crisps, though crisps and coffee is not good. We might need water. Or instead of sandwiches and crisps, a flaky pastry. I might need to have my own pastry, though. I never feel full after a croissant. Half would really not work. I'm fairly sure the paint is just entering the wood and moving around inside the wood, spreading deep into the house, making it, if anything, harder and sturdier. This is what I will say to the letting company if they raise the issue of the leaking paint and the crack that seems not to let the paint out on the other side. I do not want to think about the letting company appraising the house while I'm away. If they raise the rent or send more tenants in to fill the empty rooms, I will probably have to find somewhere else to live, and I would hate that because what if it means that I can't walk to your house any more? I prefer not to think about it. Or maybe on the holiday we will get along so well that we might think about getting a place together. I realise this will be incredibly difficult. I'm about twenty minutes away from your house where I'm now standing, right now. There is a tree with pink blossom. The sky is so blue, I'm very close to crying. I can't wait to see you. I'm still so mesmerised by the idea that we are going on holiday together. I have not left the gas on.

The paint is simply entering the structure of the property I rent, and I think that's something I can live with. I'm not going to mention the paint to you when I see you. I'm going to let it soak into the building. The paint itself is in the tall cupboard under the stairs and the pot is holding up many other pots and bricks, which in turn are holding up the fifth step on the staircase, which has split in the middle. The tin of paint has a slow leak that dribbles paint down the side of itself and into a crack in the floor of the cupboard. If anyone gives me any trouble about the paint pot, I will just tell them to fix the stairs. It was not me who broke the stairs. I am standing under a cherry tree and the blossoms are swaying like a slow and purposeful parade. The colours loop in small circles and I can see them as a procession around distant mountains. I can see them as souls leaving one world and traversing the mountain paths that lead to the next world where souls go. The paint is leaking into the house like a soul. A bright yellow sun of a soul that in fact I've given to this house where I live alone, without you, under my blankets. Can I say that to the letting agents? Probably not. I am tired of being there anyway. This holiday is really what I'm pinning all my hopes on. I'm hoping that there will be time for me to buy another pair of socks because I've only got two pairs, including the socks I'm wearing. But you won't mind. You never mind me and these stupid things I do, although you do call them stupid. I like it. Your smiling eyes when we insult each other. You say I'm an idiot (I am) and I say your cologne is awful (it's not, and it makes me absolutely drugged to smell it on you).

I'm so excited about the prospect of buying and wearing holiday socks, and drinking wine with you, and the sun going into my skin, going into my bones. I have my eyes closed. I have stopped in the street to listen to the world as it is today. I can hear people walking by. I love these people. I said I would text you before I left, but I've not done that. I'm afraid the little blue key ran out of its emergency £5-worth so there is no power at the house. So

I've not charged my phone. I've not been able to turn a light on. It's OK because there's nothing in the fridge. There is nothing in the freezer except Tupperware and ratatouille that I'm sure is poisonous by now. I cannot wait to see you and smell the cigarettes you have recently smoked. I will watch you getting ready. I will, I expect, smell the bitter end of your sleep, the backdoor-cigarette air, the cold of your black leather jacket that you will wear on this holiday for as long as you can before it becomes too much, and you remove it and are wearing holiday things: cotton, linen, materials that let you stay cool and floating. I'm now walking. The tree and the blossoms are behind me. I will not look back. I go past the corner shop where I sometimes stop to buy tobacco for you. Not today though, you have told me you do not need any tobacco. I'm fine for tobacco you have said.

I am coming to the turning, which takes me to a road only fifteen minutes away from your house. The cars here are different today – it's weird, I can't say exactly how they are different. I suppose because I have been coming this way for so long, I've got used to them being a certain way. This red car guy parks here and this white car guy parks there, but now the red and the white car are not here. It's all cars that are on the fringes of normal car colours. Pastel lilac car, a small car. I do not drive. I do not know car names. Sweet-potato coloured car, medium-sized.

I've reached the end of this road, and the cars. They are cars. Why am I thinking about cars? Why am I talking about them? Is this talking or thinking? I do not know what this is. This. It shouldn't matter. It doesn't matter.

Oh here we go. There is a sign telling me that the next road I need to take to get to your house is closed. There is a fence across the entire width of the road. There is tape on the pavements that reads GAS LEAK. There has been a gas leak. I can smell gas in the air, heavy and sweet. I've always liked the smell they add to gas. It's not really there – real methane, pure methane, is completely odourless. But the smell it has, the smell they add so you can smell it in the home, is a good smell.

I have inhaled a lot of gas. Quite harmless at this level of dilution, I feel sure. I realise again that there is no battery left on my phone, so I cannot tell you about the smell of gas. I want urgently to tell you about the particular golden colour that I see when I experience this smell, how the taste of it fills me with the idea that there will soon be food and there will be a warm kitchen, with damp on the windows right down to the spongey wood of the sill, and no way of seeing outside, and no reason to open up to the cold night. I would love for us to be together inhaling this gas, so heavy I can chew it in my mouth like sausages. I've turned around now and I'm heading back down the road I've just walked. I'm on a detour, that's all. This small bubble of anxiety I have inside me is probably just the gas, along with the excitement for the holiday. I'm fairly sure I know the way. I've got everything I need. I am not afraid.

This new road is pretty. All the doorways are quite dark. There are tall buildings, urban mansion blocks probably built in the 1930s (I know nothing about architecture but who cares), with wide balconies on the higher floors. White iron railings. I do not recognise any of them. I feel so far away, but if I turn around, I can still see the road I know, the one with the blossom and the unexpected car colours. I'm less than ten minutes away from my house, and probably only about twenty minutes away from your house. My suitcase makes a lot of noise. I'm dragging it along on its little wheels. I feel like the people are hiding on their balconies. They do not want to be seen by me, or to have to deal with the noise of my suitcase. I mention this because I don't know what else can have attracted the attention of this guy. He's young-looking, with expensive thin-framed glasses on.

'Hey,' he says. 'Hey, have you got a minute? I need some help. It's just a quick thing,' he says. 'I'm helping someone – and it's embarrassing to admit it, right, but I can't do it by myself. Can you spare a minute, mate?'

He's calling me 'mate'. I don't know what to say to this guy. He's gesturing over towards one of those dark brick mansion buildings.

'I'm late,' I've told him. I have gestured to the suitcase.

He is holding up his hands – 'Oh god!' he says. 'Of course you are. Of course you are. I'm a prick for asking. Sorry mate. You go. What is it, a flight? Fuck! Airports are a nightmare, mate. The check-in these days.'

He's talking about the check-in at the airport. I'm lost a little bit because I'm looking at him. His skin is so tight on his bald head. He has the dissociative shrunken eyes of a bear and the skin on his head must be putting some kind of structural pressure on his skull. He's still talking.

'You're there, in the check-in, longer than the actual holiday. Forget it! I'm sorry. I'll figure it out. Don't worry at all.'

He's holding his hands up. He's looking around, he looks like a child. A lost child. He's in pain. He's wincing. He doesn't move away. I don't move away.

'Look,' I'm saying, 'look – I can probably help you if it won't take long. I was walking to meet someone – then we're going on holiday. But I can get there a bit later. I'm probably a bit early . . .'

He looks shocked. He's blinking. He looks like I've given him a sweet, this little boy.

'Really?' he says. 'I don't want to make you late. It will only take a second, but I don't want to risk it. I would never forgive myself, mate, if I ruined your holiday. And whoever you're going with? Oh Jesus Christ I would kill myself if I ruined someone's holiday . . .'

'It's fine! Hey, it's fine,' I'm saying. 'Let's go. I'll help if I can . . .'

'Really? You are a saint. An angel! Bless you man.'

He has called me an angel. He has put his hand on my back. He has had his hand on my back for a second and now he's got my bag.

'What is it we're doing, then?' I ask.

'Just helping with this shed, he says . . .'

I cannot see a shed anywhere. He's got my bag. He's leading me across the road, doubling me back on myself, almost, to the dark wide doors of the mansion block from which he must have appeared. I realise I do not know the name of this road. I try to see but fail to see any number or name for the building. Usually they have names. Woodpecker Mount. Crow's Bellow. Stuff like that, but this one has no name that I can see. The open double doors have no writing on them. There is no plaque with a name on. There is no sign on the unkempt lawn.

I'm inside now, and this man is still talking. He's got my bag. The door swings shut behind me. It's dark in here. It smells of cleaning product – lemons. Trees. Bleach. I follow the man round the stairs, along a narrow corridor. It looks like a service corridor. Very clean, very dark. There is one solitary scuff mark along the wall. I find myself following the line of it – like a break in the wall, a mournful scuff. Then I'm going through the back door into a huge communal garden. The smell of gas is strong here. The man still has my bag.

The door behind me slams shut. Is this how easy it is to snatch someone off the street? I'm wondering if I've been snatched off the street by this athletic man. I think he must work in sales, or something. He looks very lean. His body fat percentage is probably about 0.1 per cent.

Of course, I've not been snatched off the street. I'm following the man through an expansive, rich garden. There are significant veins on his wrists. His hands are not huge, but they are powerful. He does hand exercises, definitely. He has a grip strength training device, I can tell. I was told I should use a grip strength training device by the doctor, a long time ago. I never actually used it. Maybe twice. My hands ached a lot afterwards, and I was meant to work and I couldn't work. I was doing data entry. The only data I could tell you about was the ache in my hands: I had to push them between my thighs and lean forward. Which looked strange. It was only a temporary job. They didn't do more than email when I stopped turning up. One email asking if I was OK. Then nothing.

Up ahead, walking through what now feels like a meadow, a wildflower meadow, the man is still pulling my suitcase, dragging it through the long, dry grass, tugging up hanks of lawn. Dirt and divots shed themselves from the underside of the case.

'Hey man,' I'm saying. 'Where's,' I say, 'where's the shed?'

'Just down here, mate. Not far. Won't take long . . .'

It feels crazy that this garden can be here and be so private. The sound of insects is so loud, so peaceful. Chubby noises, luxurious buzzing.

There is an orchard.

'Hey, is this an orchard?' I ask. I ask such stupid questions, I'm aware of this.

'Sure, pear orchard,' he says. Casual as anything. 'Take a pear if you want.'

I tell him I'm OK. I'm not ready for a pear. We are now in the centre of the orchard, and here, within the orchard, is a shed. It's a small classical-style shed. Silver wood. Felted roof that meets in a peak in the middle. The roof, I can see now, is collapsing.

'I just need you to go inside and hold up the roof,' the man says.

'OK.'

'You have to be firm, right? Otherwise it's collapse time, and we both end up in a pickle!'

'OK.'

I'm saying OK. I'm not asking how long this will take. The smell – I do in fact mean fragrance – of this field is astonishing to me. The man is talking again.

'Don't worry,' he is saying. 'While you hold it up, I'm gonna nip up and refresh that felt. Takes about five minutes. Then I should be done. Then it should basically be finished. And you will be hasta la vista, right? Gone with the wind.'

As I'm being ushered towards the door, the man continues mumbling about how he should at last be finished, and that he had surely done enough. And something about 'fucking powder everywhere'.

'Fucking powder,' he just said, but he's gone now, I'm alone in the dark now. I'm inside this shed. My arms ache. It's itchy too, in the dark, there are insects on my wrists, irritating. I can't scratch, I can't do anything because then it'll be collapso time for the shed and I will be crushed.

I wonder if I should feel so angry with myself for allow-ing this to happen, but he is out there. He sounds like he is making progress.

'I'm putting my weight on the roof now,' he says. 'Don't drop me!'

I am holding all of his weight above me now. I can feel him moving around up there, and I'm straining under the weight of him. He's applying glue. It's strange how he feels as he moves around, like being under a blanket with a cat above me.

He says he is nearly finished. He says it about five times. My arms are burning.

'There was a tear in the felting,' he says, appearing at the door. 'Pain in the ass. Rain got in.'

I am still holding the roof up. I'm shaking. I'm wondering if this will show up on the beach, this last-minute bit of exercise. Have I got a beach body now? No. I shall be keeping all this firmly hidden on the beach. I shouldn't be criticising myself. I'm holding up a shed and I'm doing this to myself. You hate it when I criticise myself. I'm holding up a shed.

The man is back. He tells me, 'You can let go now, mate. Thanks for your help.'

He has taken the weight of the shed roof from me with just one arm. He is banging nails into it. The wood is spitting and groaning where he bangs in his nails. I escape from under his hot armpit and go outside.

I wait among the pear trees and think of the beach and being so warm, so warm that I forget what it was like in bed last night, the damp and the cold and that dribbling sound.

'Thanks again, mate!' the man has said. He is now walking back towards the house. I tell him it's no problem at all, though he thanked me maybe thirty seconds or so ago.

He's way ahead of me now, he's reached the door of the building. Why is he storming off? I was expecting more backslapping and thank yous and blessings. And my bag, my fucking holiday bag! I'm back in the building, I ran here, and wait – what? He's going upstairs!

'Hey man. I need my bag!' I call up.

'Yeah in a sec mate,' he calls back. 'We have to sort some stuff out upstairs.'

'I need to go,' I say.

'Won't take long,' comes this man's sing-song reply. 'Then I'll be done with this fucking place.'

I think that's what he has just said. My memories seem to be washing away faster than they come. It's a tide, every wash, I forget. I am recording as much as I can in this way. Whatever this is.

'This fucking place,' he has definitely said that. His voice is quiet now because he's so high up. He's still going. He's still going. He's spiralling out of sight up the stairs with my black trundling holdall. It's got everything in it. I want to leave it here, and just come to you and have breakfast and ask to borrow some socks and maybe buy a few essentials from the train station, or the second train station (I've remembered there are two trains we must get. Train one is slow and train two is fast. On train one we will be tense, and it rattles along but will be so crowded. On the second train, the more luxurious train, we will relax. Oh, we will have pastry! I want to be on the trains! I'm refusing to contemplate missing the trains. I can see you. I can see the words of you on the trains. My stomach leaps for you. Like a switch, just thinking of you).

I could raid the holiday budget, I think. Get everything I need from the airport shop. It would make you angry. To be honest, you would be right to be angry.

We enter a flat through a heavy green iron door on the top floor. The man seems out of place here. This dusty flat, full of fabrics, smells of mothballs. There's no way this guy lives here. This guy wouldn't even take off his coat in this room, I don't think. He wouldn't eat off the plates or drink from the cups. He definitely would not remove his shoes – but I like it. I mean, I wish I weren't here, but also I left early, and I'm still thinking this will be a good story to tell you. On the list of times – the itinerary – I have in my head, we are now approaching the time I would have arrived if there had been no gas leak, no shed to fix, or this flat.

I'm acknowledging that this actually would have been too early. I would have arrived and maybe frustrated your preparations. You would have let me in and made me a cup of tea and then left me to drink it while you went off to shower and go about your business.

'What's going on?' I'm asking the man. 'Why have you brought me up here?'

'I'm sorry, mate, but I've actually lied to you,' he says. He is striding around the mess of the flat, occasionally touching his very bald head. 'There's actually a little bit more to do.' There are some beads of sweat on the skin over his temples. Is he agitated because his skin is slowly killing him by suffocation of the skull bones?

'You lied to me?' I'm saying. I sound confused, I think, rather than furious, which is of course how I feel. I want to attack him. Or at the very least grab my bag and run away, but no. Instead, here it comes. Here comes the adrenaline in my stomach. Here comes the paralysis. Fight or flight, that's meant to be the reaction, but I just stand here. No fight. No flight. All I can think is that I wish you were here. We would laugh and walk away.

'You lied to me?' I've said it again. I sound like someone who has been folded up and put into a pocket.

'Yeah, just a little one. It's not just the shed, there's this lot as well. This whole place. Twenny max,' he says. 'Twenny.'

Twenny! I'm numb. I can't believe I'm now actually doing maths. I think it will be OK. I will arrive just before you start worrying about me.

I should ask for money, that's what I should do. But it feels shameful to lower myself like that. I can be bought? No. But apparently I can simply be coerced and diverted from my business. You can lead me by the hand into a prison, and I won't ask for a penny.

The man is gathering the books into piles that are leaning all over the floor of this nice but faded apartment. He grabs a pile of books and dumps it into a box. 'Crack on, then!' he says.

I'm grinding my teeth. I've so much adrenaline sloshing in me. I'm a statue. I'm in the middle of the living room of this flat. Between the piles of books, I can see that the floor itself is a high-quality surface. It could be a floor in an office in a French 1950s television studio. Dark, hard, old vinyl, impervious to shoes and machismo.

It's very dusty in here. Mud-brown curtains cover the large windows. These windows must open out onto one of the balconies I saw from the road, but I can't see any way to access the windows themselves, or doors, or French windows or whatever.

The man in glasses has found a rhythm now. He is hurriedly stack-ing books into boxes. His breathing comes heavily, as though he has decided to approach this task like he's at the gym. He's con-trolling his form, I can see, using his core to focus the rapid movement of piles of books into boxes, his feet flat on the floor, operating in and out of deep, grunting squats. 'Fuckssake,' he's hissing through his tightly controlled breath. 'Fucks-sake,' which he probably means as one level up from 'Crack on.'

I'm not meant to be here. I squat down and pick up a pile of books – heavy, slippery and instantly tiring. I put them in a box. The titles in the pile I have are not easy to read. They seem to be reference books. The words swim. I do not know what they say. One is the colour of sweetcorn, with small black writing.

On another pile, the top book has a faded picture of a grand-father in a checked shirt being handed a note by a granddaughter with a huge smile on her face.

The man does not seem impressed that I've started helping. I pick up another pile. 'No – not those ones,' he says. 'I'm doing those ones. Help with something else. Diana!'

He's suddenly shouting 'Diana'!

Inevitably, Diana arrives from another room. My instincts tell me that the room Diana has just been in is a bedroom. She looks as if she has been lying down.

'You're from the agency,' Diana asks me, although she doesn't really ask me. She tells me.

She looks so tired, this Diana. It makes me think of you, when you sometimes fall asleep in your work clothes. I'm thinking of you now. I can see you going around the rooms, getting ready for our holiday. Can I? No, not actually see you. I can hear the words I myself am saying now, these words describing you. Am I saying words? Whatever this is. You are there in your flat, going around. A lovely way of walking inside rooms, you have. Amazing when you come into a room.

I'm looking forward to telling you all about this. I'm running late now. Not really late, but I'm no longer massively early, which I had planned to be.

I think we have missed the first cup of tea we would have had. I think the second cup of tea will become the first cup of tea now, and over the second cup of tea (now the first cup of tea), I will tell you all of this. I try to see the details as much as I can, as many of them as I can, so I can describe them to you.

For example, the details of Diana's hands, the way they are moving as she shows me around, explaining things to me. I am not paying attention to her words. I'm doing this in my head. What is this for god's sake? This. This talking I'm doing now. I am doing this. I'm thinking about telling you about Diana. Her hands move very precisely through the air. It's impressive how she moves them – she could be an orchestra conductor.

For some reason, Diana's arrival has made me feel much more relaxed. When it was just me and the man with glasses (I still do not know his name) I was afraid. I felt trapped here. In fact, I feel that I was taken against my will. Kidnapped? Maybe I was! I was kidnapped, but now Diana's here and it feels much more like a job I'm doing. Some temp thing.

It's just another shift I'm going to excuse myself from early because the work is dreadfully boring and I want to be with you.

Yes, I feel able to get out of this situation whenever I like, and then easily find my way to you and to our cup of tea. Or if we don't have time for tea, then just some water. I'm thinking now that you may not want to put the kettle on again at this time. You will want to leave very early for the airport. You will want to spend at least three hours in the waiting area after we have got through security. You will want us both to have a pint of lager there. I, too, want this. I want the holiday to start as early as it can, but now I think I will have a story to tell you and we will unpack these events together on the train, or the second train, or in the bar at the airport.

I've zoned back into what Diana is saying. We are no longer in the main living space. The man with glasses has stopped whatever he was doing with boxes. I can no longer hear him. I'm in a bedroom. The room is lit by small lamps somewhere near the oblong of the bed, or at least I have to assume it's a bed. This room feels very long, like a hall. Very long and narrow. The walls are such a dark green it's almost black. The jumper you got in the sales in January, the dark green one – the walls look like that. A wet forest at night. The floor is the same heavy, tough plastic.

I'm helping Diana find something to wedge the door open. The door refuses to stay open. It's not a heavy door or anything. You can open it easily like any door. But for some reason, as soon as you let go, it starts to close.

This is the bedroom of Russel Palomet. I have this information in my mind without being told who Russel Palomet is. Nobody has spoken this name. Diana is still trying to pick things up to put in front of the door, but she does not seem able to pick anything up. I can't help her because I'm focused on the name Russel Palomet, which is now inside my head. In here with us both – you and me and Russel Palomet.

I close my eyes and breathe, and the darkness of having my eyes closed has changed. My personal darkness, the specific way it looks to me when I close my eyes, has changed. Clouds of thin grey mist have entered my darkness. The floating dots of purple and red that I'm accustomed to seem trapped in the grey mist. The grey mist is Russel Palomet. You can't see him, but the bit of you that can hear this, can hear me, can see him. We are in the dark, and our sky is being invaded by the cold cloud of this man we do not know and have not seen in human form.

This room tapers into a grey space in the corners. I feel like I am inside a duvet cover.

'Russel Palomet must be watched now,' Diana says.

'I can't see him,' I say. 'I'm meant to be somewhere.'

Diana doesn't acknowledge that I'm meant to be somewhere. 'It's not necessary to see him in order to watch him,' she says.

'I have to go,' I say. I say it so quietly, so meekly, that Diana glares at me.

'Don't forget to complete your time sheet. You must complete your time sheet immediately at the end of your shift.'

'Diana,' I say, 'you know that I'm not actually here for work. I don't have a time sheet.'

'If we don't receive the time sheet in time, you will forfeit your double pay. I have to go.'

The way Diana says 'I have to go' is much more complete than the way I've been saying it. I want to shove Diana (as gently as I can) out of the way and rush out of this room and get the hell out of this flat, but of course I cannot. My legs won't do it. I close my eyes; the grey mist is everywhere. I worry about you in there, in my darkness, waiting for me, covered in that cloud.

Diana tells me to turn around.

'I'm not sure I can, actually, Diana,' I say.

'Just fucking turn around, please. Turn your back to me.'

I turn around. I can turn around but I can't leave. This is classic. Why does this shit happen to me, I'm asking you, but you can't hear me. Not even the you that I keep in my head can hear me complaining about this.

Diana is stripping. I can hear her removing her clothes.

Diana is removing her clothes. I try to think about this as a real situation. I resolve not to close my eyes again. In the realness of the situation, I cannot wait to tell you about all of the things that are happening to me right now. If I ever see you again. But of course I will see you again. As soon as Diana leaves the room, presumably in different clothes, I will leave too. I'll give it a bit of time and then I'll go. I'll tell her that Russel Palomet told me it was fine.

'Can I turn back yet?'

'No,' Diana says. 'I'm nude.'

'Why are you nude, Diana?'

'Spores,' she says. Nothing else. Spores. This is too much. I've been kidnapped by her and she's talking about spores. I need to get out and call the police and explain that I've been kidnapped by a supervisor of some kind and a man with medically overtight skin. I need to be driven to the airport immediately.

Quite a long time passes, and I realise that Diana is about to leave the room and leave me in here with Russel Palomet. I turn around just as Diana's naked back and arm vanish through the door.

The door closes with a short click. Diana's smart black suit is on the floor in a heap. I stoop to look at the heap of Diana's clothes. There definitely does seem to be a sort of powder on the fabric. A powder the colour of pollen, but darker, muddier. I kick the clothes away and spores rise up with a sighing sound. A sound like disappointment.

My hands are shaking a little bit now. You would be rolling your eyes at me. You would have rolled your eyes at me nonstop since I woke up this morning. I wanted to come to your place last night but you said you wanted to have some time to yourself. You rolled your eyes at me when I tried to convince you. You rolled them and sighed and said, 'No, go home, I'll see you tomorrow.' I smiled and we hugged, but you must have known that I felt ridiculous. I feel ridiculous all the time. I wonder if you can hear me. Am I talking to you? What is this? What is this that I'm doing? Sometimes it makes sense and then suddenly I don't know what I'm doing. Is it talking? What is this? The room is like a cotton bin bag. The room is a church collection bag. The room is the sack that Mr Moore kept the throwing bean bags in for PE. I have to get out of this room. The spores smell of lavender and sick.

I open the door, but it doesn't open.

I cannot open the door. I bang on the door but I cannot bang on the door. It makes no sound. My hands do not make contact with anything. I try to bang the door again but I can't touch it. My hand reaches the surface of the door, and just as I am about to make impact, there is no impact. I shout, 'I need to leave!' but, of course, there is no reply.

Somewhere in here is Russel Palomet. I can sense the presence of this person.

'Russel Palomet,' I say. 'Please allow me to leave this room.'

'Certainly,' says the voice of Russel Palomet. It is a soft voice, like big petals – flouncy tulips or roses, those petals that, when they are just ready, you touch them against your lips (I've seen you do this many times).

I try to open the door again but the same thing happens. I am somehow unable to even touch the door.

'That won't work,' says the voice of Russel Palomet. 'You are too passive now. Please don't be alarmed, it is only temporary.'

I think about your response to me being called passive. Your knowing look, even though I'm now passive on an atomic level, rather than just being a pushover. Your smirking face at my atomic deterioration. Your little smile.

I'm being unfair. I think you would probably be helping me if you were here. You would be saying, this is not your fault, Ben. You are kind, that's all. You say good things about me regularly. I don't know why, when I talk to you like this, I make you sound so unforgiving. I make you sound cruel, but actually, this is me being cruel, underplaying you.

'But you said I could leave,' I plead with Russel Palomet. 'I'm supposed to be somewhere. I'm supposed to go on holiday.'

I'm saying all of this with a shaking voice. 'The person I'm going with is waiting. They will be at home now going frantic. Have you got a phone?'

'No phone.'

'A computer?'

'No computer.'

There's nothing. I've been kidnapped and left in a state of abject passiveness. I can see you now on the train, muttering under your breath. Going to the airport. You are furious, but also determined to enjoy your holiday. On the plane, still in your heavy jacket. You will still be in that jacket, right up until the moment you are in the hotel room.

'I'm going to move on you now,' Russel Palomet says. The words are in my head. I've still not seen Russel Palomet. 'I'm moving on you now. It is not my intention that you find this uncomfortable, but if it is, I won't stop, I'm afraid. I'm moving on you now. The particles of me are in between the particles of you. Look, I'm going to drink a glass of orange juice, and you will taste orange juice. It will be hard for you to speak or respond now for a while. I am Russel Palomet and I am on you completely. I've no intention of making this feel like an invasion, or what have you, but I'm aware it is a violation, of course. An imposition. I'm going to drink some more orange juice. I love orange juice. I'm going to go downstairs. You won't be able to move but you will feel the impact of going downstairs. I'm in a celebrated European city. When I emerge from the stairwell, it will be into a dark corridor. It is hundreds of years old, this building. Merchants — so many merchants — have lived here. Have occupied this place. I live here. Nobody knows about me. I live here and I drink orange juice. Sometimes I drink coffee or I go for a run on the running machine. Right now I'm on the street. There is a canal beside me — oh, it's beautiful. I think you can see it, the sunlight on the cold water, how it dances, how it tells you how cold it is. The sheer light means it is absolutely freezing in there. I'm heading along the street now. I'm going to speak to someone who sells antiques. I'm going to walk very quickly. Tourists, so many tourists — they walk slowly. They are on drugs. They are pathetic. I barged a young boy out of the way just then, did you feel that? A teen. Stupid kid, he looks terrified. God knows what he is experiencing right now. I guess he should try being you, hey! Oh sorry, I think that was probably insensitive. I'm sorry, but I really do get overexcited and cross with all these tourists. Motherfucking pricks. He'll be fine, that kid. He has already forgotten, I expect.

//Russel Palomet! Please stop this!//

No. No I won't. That kid. I won't stop, did you see him? He's just back to having a good time. He's just a mushroom. Do you know what I'm buying from this antiques dealer? A hot bed pan. It's something I like. I have always liked them – you fill the shallow copper bowl with hot coals and embers.

//I am trying to stop Russel Palomet but I feel weaker than anything. Weaker than smoke. I try to see you. Or say the words that make you visible. You are not yet on the train. You are leaving soon. You have a face. I love you.//

You put a lid on and then – it's on the end of a long stick, right, I will imagine one and you will see it. You see it? So you put the embers in that copper bowl at the end. Then, holding the stick, you slip the bowl into the bed, in between the sheets, and then you slowly move it left to right, up and down, like that. It's this action I like the best: you slip it between the sheets and move it around. On boiled-crisp white sheets. There is nothing on earth as satisfying as sliding a hot bed pan around on boil-crisp white sheets. Then you put it somewhere safe, where it won't burn the fucking house down, and you quickly get into bed. It feels like someone was just there. Like someone just got up and they let you have their space in the bed. It's an amazing feeling, and this dealer has got an excellent one. I'm nearly at his shop. I love this man's shop. His co-owner is here – she is a brilliant antiques dealer. This is great. I am talking to them. We're old friends, we're going to the back room. I'm going to drink some wine now. Delicious. You can taste the wine, I hope, and you can sense the feeling of joy I have in the company of these excellent dealers. I feel bad, so I tell them about the boy I shoved earlier. They say they understand. Is all of this going too fast for you? I get the sense that you are struggling with all this. You keep thinking about other things. You keep thinking about going on holiday. You should let go of that. My wine tastes of salt! Stop this now. I'm going to squeeze your particles. I won't allow you to ruin this for me. Can you feel that? I'm sorry. I realise you probably feel very sick, but you can't be sick any more, you are far too passive for sick.

I am going to drink some more wine, and then, later, I'm sorry to say, I will go out drinking heavily with these guys, and with some other friends. I'm sorry, but this will be a long day. I'm definitely hoping that the co-owner of the antiques shop will take us all dancing. She loves dancing. She insists on dancing whenever she can. She moves like a moon attached to several other moons, and I find it absolutely captivating.

You are interfering again, I can tell. You're feeding me sunshine and sand. I don't want sand. I don't want this presence with us, who is this? This figure with us, who is this? They smell of tobacco. Why are they wearing a leather jacket on the beach? Why do I love them? This is you. Stop it. If you don't stop it I will tear you. I can do that, you know?

I'm going out with my friends. We're going to get intimate at least once with this one particular friend. The moons of her head and her various body moons, and my body moons, too, moving to the music, bouncing people away, clearing space, eating. We will eat so much food. And, later, several of us will go to a hotel with giant beds. I'm warming the beds now. It has been hours — they will have passed you by because I've torn you. You are just standing there, in that bedroom where you claim to have been kidnapped. Trying to make me think of your holiday, your kebabs and lager. Your sweet apple juice breakfast and stupid holding hands in the shade.

This isn't about you! You're ruining it. Just stay where you are so I can get into these hot beds with these other horny antiques enthusiasts. It's not much to ask, is it? I will never get to do this again. This is my final moment.

I'm sorry. I can tell that your legs are tired. Some areas of your being, certain areas, I'm afraid, will not be easily repaired. I've damaged you. It happens. You won't notice. Hours are going by. A whole day has gone by for me, and for you, standing there, in that room, days are slipping away.

It doesn't seem fair. I've torn you. I'm sorry. I want you to know I'm sorry. I am really enjoying myself. The day has passed exactly as I said it would and I am very happy. I'm warming a bed that is a super emperor bed – there are several beautiful antiques dealers in here. We're going to have a hot bed.

It's the morning – I'm eating bacon in the hotel lobby. I am miserable. The night ended too soon.

I fell asleep and someone was arguing, I don't remember who, but they argued and I woke up alone and frustrated. I'm eating bacon and drinking a pint of orange juice. I've torn you completely and I'm not sorry.'

The voice of Russel Palomet has stopped. There is only the cloud now, the cloud of him. I believe he is dissipating. The walls of this bedroom are soaking wet. The spores that were on Diana's crumpled black suit have turned into mushy masses the size of tennis balls. They are oozing. The smell is horrific. I feel exhausted.

I open the door.

I am on the street.

I have no choice but to go home. I've missed the holiday. I've missed everything. I had no say in any of this. My house, I remember, has no electricity, and so it will be freezing cold. All my money is in euros. I know it will be impossible to get the electricity on, but I have no choice.

The smell of gas has gone. It's all normal traffic pollution again.

I'm passing the blossoms on the tree. They have gone over, now. Most of the petals are on the floor, soaked and mashed into the pavement. There is fox shit hanging out of a bottle of Yop. The cars are awful colours. I am dragging my suitcase behind me. You are gone.

There are people outside the house. I am probably being evicted. There is a man in a suit. He must be from the letting agency. And there is someone else there, too. I do not know who the other person is. My house, I can see from here, is shimmering somehow. Is it burning? No, the house is not burning. I can't see properly. My eyes do not work. But there is a shape of someone at my door. It is you! You are there at my door, you are banging, hammering on the door, about to crack it open like the dog-yellow shell of an egg.

The door in the back of Simon's head

'Hey, drink this!'

Jonty was offering me a tube containing a liquid. I gave it a look.

'It's an essential part of the celebrations,' he said. I continued to stare at the liquid. This was not a good thing to be drinking, I thought, but Jonty almost never looked at me like this, like I was part of something.

'What's going on?' I asked him.

'It's happening,' Jonty said, with glazed eyes. 'Simon can accommodate us. And when I say "us", I mean the entire workforce.'

So that explained it, we were finally going to enter the door in the back of Simon's head. I'd noticed the door there, just above his nape, on the day I joined. A little wooden-looking door, with a round knob. I'd seen it as a surprising growth, nothing more. I'd never spoken of the door, though Simon knew we stared.

He once caught me raising my hand up to it, about to knock.

Simon was a wispy presence in the office, really. Apart from his door, an unremarkable man. Long ago he'd been a brilliant systems architect, but now he was a spent force. Hired for dependability over dynamism.

As he drifted past the glass meeting room, he did not look like someone who'd agreed to have everyone in the office enter his head through the door above his neck. He looked like someone who was rerunning an argument with his partner, a quiet habit.

I wondered how this agreement had come about. I pictured Jonty with his arm around Simon at some ill-advised after-hours drinks, berating him, disregarding all forms of decency, insisting that he be granted access.

'Drink,' Jonty said again. 'I've seen you looking at it too. You want to go as much as I do.'

Jonty gestured out towards Simon's desk, as though he was not a man at all, but some area of town.

I drank the liquid in the tube. The meeting ended.

The day passed in a breathless series of lurching bodily changes. I sensed that the whole company had become much less rigid in our atomic structure. The view through the windows had frayed. Enormous gaps appeared in everything that had once seemed solid.

I now saw Simon's door as a destination.

'What do you think it will be like?' I asked Tonia, the office manager.

She whispered that she had already been in there to perform health and safety checks. 'There is a free bar,' she explained, 'in our area.'

'Our area?'

Tonia seemed pleased that I had asked. 'The whole interior of the head has been organised into areas. In some areas are his mother giving lectures, or his early experiences of life. There are several species of bird. We must only go to our allocated area.'

'How long will we be inside?' I asked, but Tonia was now fully engaging with the door in Simon's head – using her lanyard to gain access. I took a breath, and wondered how I would perceive colour inside Simon's head.

I wondered if I would ever see my partner again, and, as I reached the threshold of Simon's skull, and looked up at the now vast oak door, I felt a rush of yearning to be at home, sipping tea that was cold, being asked if I would mind sweeping the leaves in the garden.

A conversation near a window

I will always remember how bright the sun was shining at the time of my short holiday in the village by the sea. I forget the name of the village. It was not Polperro, but it was similar. It is no longer possible for me to check.

I can tell you that the days I spent on my holiday were filled with an endless light. Wherever I went – to the little pub garden for lunch, or down to the stone harbour to look at the cold ocean, or into the village to consider the shops selling crystals – all I wanted was to drape myself in the light. I felt that it was charging me up, all that radiance. It wasn't even very warm, not summer sun at all, but a light that had a physical power to touch me, to energise my pores and my bones.

In the evenings, I continued to feel the charge of this light, even though the sky was moonless and clouded. I felt as though I had batteries that would last forever. I became charming. Or at least, I certainly felt as though I was being charming to all I met. I had a drink with a man, he put his arm around me. I could smell him, he smelt of whisky but also of soap and his lips were enormous and soft. I pictured him kissing me. I pictured waking up with his giant pink head on the white pillow next to mine. He talked to me for a long time about a colony of ants he had kept as a boy. I was very charming to this man. I was charming to his wife and to his three adult sons who all gazed at me, I think, with longing.

At night I slept, alone, inside dreams of a golden state. I woke each day without even a trace of tiredness or dehydration. It was an amazing holiday. I was alone the whole time, and yet also present in crowds of people, treated like a dignitary. Left alone when I made it politely clear I wanted to return to my thoughts. Perfect, really, perfect.

You can imagine the slump in my spirits when I had to return to work. I hadn't been back more than two days before the light charge had completely worn off.

On the third day, I received a call from my doctor, insisting that I should come in for a conversation.

Come today, if you can, she said. This afternoon.

What's a conversation? I asked. What does this mean, a conversation?

She explained that a conversation was not the same as a surgery consultation. She told me about successful pilot studies in which conversations have been used in place of full-blown consultations.

I tried to detect clues as to what might be the problem with my health.

It's not normal for a doctor to call you up, I said. Even if it is for a conversation.

Oh it is now, she said. These days a conversation is really the best thing for everybody.

So it's nothing specific? I said. I shouldn't be worried?

No, not worried, no. You should just come in and see me very soon. Today really.

I realised that all the time I had been on the phone, I had been walking aimlessly around the office. I came to a stop near the recycling and confidential waste bins. I looked at the people around me. I saw Rianne going into the small client conference booth to make her update call to New York.

I pictured the meetings in my own calendar that would now be cancelled while I went to the doctor for my conversation. I mourned them, these meetings for the healthy: a nice one with the marketing team, always very civilised, mostly just a chance to catch up. Nice scenes of casual holiday chat, of biscuits and coffee from the coffee place on the street came to me and blew away again like smoke.

I felt burdened suddenly, as though a great debt rested on my shoulders, which of course it did, but that was not the trouble. I was sick.

The doctor was talking still, I was making polite noises about how interesting it all sounded, and listening to her trying to get Outlook to open on her computer.

I felt sure that something was very wrong, and I looked again at the people in the office. There was Sam going to Katarina's desk, leaning there, the two of them smiling, saying things, invisible things. The tangibility of these people put me on edge. I had the inescapable impression that I was encased in webbing of some kind, and that this webbing was pulling me away from Sam and Katarina.

Are you free this afternoon? repeated the doctor's voice. She sounded rather desperate in fact, which troubled me. I said I was free.

Good, don't worry, she said. She sounded relieved. Come in for a conversation and then we can get a handle on things.

I asked what things? But she had hung up. I was speaking to nobody when I said what things. Only Sam saw me: he saw me say what things. Then he looked away and began doing his usual stretches. Sam liked to stretch in the middle of the office. He was revealing his arms, which were tanned and long. He held his forearms out in front of himself as he stretched some well-honed muscles in an area of his back. Sam was covered in muscles. He always needed to stretch them, and look at himself. He went to another desk to talk to someone else.

I want to say that he had a tail, but of course he did not have a tail.

These things have become blurred.

I walked back to my desk. I saw that it was only 10.15 and time for my catch-up meeting with Declan, the assistant to the CFO.

I went to the meeting room, as usual. Declan came in and we said hello and I began describing how I could help the finance office with their internal newsletter – You need more structure, I explained. It's quite simple, I said. You're not writing a whodunnit. You can tell people the best news right at the top of the page. You don't need a big reveal.

Declan seemed not to hear me. He was absorbed in his own smiling. The meeting room was made of glass. Declan stared out, across the office. There was a sorrowful look within his smile.

Such nice people, he began to say. I guess you can't ask for anything more.

He leant back in his chair and gestured to them again. Lovely people, he said.

In the dining-slash-play area Eloise and Katarina were battling out the semifinal of the latest intra-office ping-pong tournament. A few watchers had gathered. Katarina was a former pro tennis player, and Eloise had won medals in squash in recent years. It was close, but, as Declan and I watched, it became clear that Katarina's professional training, the hard-wired need to win, would carry it for her. The flow of perfect smashes came too thick for Eloise to handle. She began to make errors. Katarina, always smiling, gave no quarter.

Lovely people, and such hard workers, Declan said.

Yeah, I know what you mean, I said, unable to think of anything else.

We watched the game in silence for a while, and then I remember distinctly that when I looked back towards Declan, after a long rally had ended, his face and head rapidly became a walnut right before my eyes, the skin wrinkling, hardening. A dry sound emanating from within the head as this occurred, the sound of something completely irreversible. He seemed conscious and aware of the world around him while his head became a walnut.

Declan, I said. He did not reply, but looked at me.

We sat with his walnutting for a moment. He touched his face, gasping a little as he explored the new contours he had. His eyes, on rigid stalks, were layered with a kind of papery rind: his new eyelids. They made a hushing sound as he blinked.

Declan, I said.

I couldn't think of anything else to say at all. He had just been musing about how nice everyone was, and now this! *This* was his life now. He was a walnut head – and that's how he would have to go home to his family. When his mother called for their Mother's Day video chat, he would have to present her with a walnut head. His children would get driven to swimming lessons by a walnut head. His partner would have to tenderly caress his walnut head. Of course, we could never call it that. We could never call it a wal-nutting. Nor could we call Declan a walnut head. Not to his face. Not out loud.

In all office settings, the event would have to be given its medical name. A code-sounding name – Syndrome BER-21 – something like that. Declan would have to overcome his need to call it a walnut head too; which, I thought at the time, is just another burden on his shoulders.

Declan and I spent a further moment in silence. Of course, I wanted to say something – even to mouth sorry – but I couldn't get there. The best I could manage was to look into his wood-coloured eyes and, at the appropriate time, blink, nod and turn my face down to my hands on the desk.

The meeting finished. I left him where he was, alone with his thoughts, looking at his non-walnut hands with his very walnut eyes.

Several minutes later, I sent him an email promising to raise a ticket for several major areas to improve the finance team's inter-nal content.

It was overkill – nobody is interested in the quality of the finance team's internal content – but I wanted to do something for Declan. Declan himself remained in the glass meeting room, slowly moving his new head, scanning the office.

I tried to imagine what he was thinking. Perhaps he was hoping someone would tell him it was reversible, or that it had happened to an uncle or a sister of a friend of theirs, and everything just calmed down after a few days. Or for someone to tell him that it hadn't happened at all, but it had.

Or rather, as I said, this is what I remember happening.

You may say otherwise.

When I looked back after sending several more emails, mostly cancelling afternoon meetings so I could attend my appointment with the doctor, I saw Declan hurrying towards the lifts, putting his jacket on as he went. Most of the people in the office watched him in stunned silence.

At the doctor's I was very nervous. I had arrived early. My hands were sweating in the waiting room. I was surrounded by children, as many as three of them, playing with the beads-on-the-wire game. I do not know, even now, why I chose that place to sit. I wanted more than anything to be alone and quiet.

I wanted time to rationalise my doctor's need for a conversation with me. I wanted to smooth out the day, and – if possible – smooth out Declan's ridged head. But no: I had not observed the first rule of waiting rooms, which is, of course, to never sit next to the balls-on-a-wire kids' game table.

This way, the receptionist said. At first, I couldn't tell if she had said my name, but she was looking right at me, and had come out from behind her desk.

Me? I said, feeling a little foolish. The children had looked up from their game.

She's been calling you for a long time, one of them said. It was the oldest of the two. A boy in blue shorts with sun cream thick on his nose and front teeth that were the size of gravestones in his mouth.

I followed the receptionist, apologising as I went. She gestured with her hand not to worry as she walked ahead of me. Her thin peach cardigan swung lazily behind her as she walked. I wondered if this was the millionth time, perhaps, that she had made this journey. A milestone of some kind.

We arrived at the doctor's door before I could say anything about the number of times she must have to get out from behind reception.

'Here,' she said.

'I wanted to ask,' I began. But she was gone already, and even though she definitely heard me in a physical human sense, she had not heard me in an administrative sense. As far as administration was concerned, I had not spoken.

The door was open a crack. Inside was the brightness of the sun. I recalled my doctor's magnificent French windows, which I had seen many times, beyond which she had a little kitchen garden, with a high brick wall and an apple tree in the corner. The light from the sun intensified as I entered the room. My doctor was sitting in her usual place, in a loose armchair by the French window. Her desk and computer were hidden out of view, around a corner. We would go there later, I realised, to enter details and make our next appointment.

Have a seat, my doctor said. I sat on a worn leather chair that squeaked expensively (vintagely) as I sank into it.

Tell me, has anything happened today? she said. Are you feeling all right?

I told her I had just got back from holiday.

Tell me about your holiday.

So I told her about my holiday. I explained how I had been, as I saw it, powered up by the sun's dazzling light. I had been a radiant friend to the locals in the evenings, and the world's most tranquil dreamer after dark. I left out the erotics of the mouths of certain big men I noticed there, because that was probably just left-over juice from the healing powers of the sun. I just happened to see the big fleshy mouth of a couple of large men, and it connected with this run-off energy. It could have been anything. Some sea-weed. A gull.

What about the daytime? she asked. She looked like she knew something about my daytimes that I did not.

Oh, not much, I said. Pub, harbour, crystals in the village. That sort of thing.

How did you get there? she asked.

Oh, you know, I said. The ah – the normal way.

All right, she said. I detected a little note of weariness in her voice. She blinked, encouraging me to keep talking.

When I was there, I went walking, I said. It was the perfect weather. I wore short sleeves and short bottoms and canvas shoes.

That sounds very relaxing.

Deck shoes, I said. Do they still call them that?

I think so. What else, what else about the holiday?

I got the sunshine!

That's good, she said.

There followed a lull. My back started to ache a little bit. I wriggled and got comfortable in the chair. I looked at the books on her shelf. They were all the same as usual: many books about parenthood, many books about experiments, social experiments.

She also had books about the human body, several large blue books about loss, and several orange books about a healthy mind-set.

After I had looked at the books on the shelves, I felt my eyes snapping into my doctor's gaze. She was wearing so many performances of beige and grey, it was hard to see the garments themselves, only several long, cooling, flowing layers. I felt very tight and blotchy suddenly, even though, as I have mentioned, I had recently been at my most radiant and graceful.

Without being asked, I started telling her about my day. I revealed that Sam had a tail, which she accepted. There have been several medical examples of tails, she said. It's unusual, but *the human tailed* are more numerous than one might think.

We decided that Sam should be proud of his tail positivity. I agreed. Sam was generally a positive person, very fit, constantly flexing in some way.

We talked around in circles for a while then, about how much more accepting society is of these different bodies.

She asked me if there was anything else on my mind. She asked me if I knew why I was there. I felt as though she was daring me now. She had shifted her position in her chair. She leant forward, challenging me to talk about Declan's walnut head.

I refused to speak.

Nothing to say at all? she said. Nothing else has happened recently?

No.

I see, she said.

We remained in a stubborn silence for a while. Something on the sun's side of things must have ignited – on the surface of the sun I mean – because the next moment the light became even more dazzling than before. I gasped at the intensity of the light. My doctor too was momentarily taken aback. The bloom pitched up, peaked, and before it could blind us both, faded back to a more manageable and pleasant level.

All my reticence faded away. I felt that surge of power come over me once more. I was once again fully charged with light.

I opened up, instantly. I told my doctor all about Declan's wal-nutted head. She nodded as I spoke, because she understood how sudden and appalling it had been. She shook her head at times too, agreeing that it was very sad. But I realised, of course, that she did not mean sad for Declan: she meant sad for me. A head cannot and does not walnut in this way. Sam might have a tail, but nobody has a walnut head. But Declan did have one. He was, right at that moment, explaining to his oldest child that things would be different, but that it would be all right somehow. That the family would struggle on together.

There's nothing that can be done for him, I said at last. At least, that's how it seems.

No, she said in a leaden voice. Nothing can be done.

We seemed to have spoken about everything that could be spoken about. I still didn't understand the difference between a conversation and a surgery consultation.

It was over. I rose from my chair, turned and headed for the door, saying thank you as I went, but the door was locked.

I think there's a mistake, I said, turning back to the doctor, but she had gone. Her voice came from round the corner, where her desk and her computer were.

No mistake, she said. Use the other door.

But – that's just your walled garden, I said.

Use the other door, she said again, this time she sounded like someone else. Someone very dry indeed.

Imagining that there must be some garden exit, I went outside through the French doors.

I stood and looked at the wall, I looked at the trees, and then all at once, I felt it rushing down upon me, the soaring, unhinged galaxy of light, and then all of them were here reaching down to me, all the walnut heads, all so beautiful and crazy and streaming with imagination.

Exit interview for a Valued Colleague

You asked if we are recording this. The answer is yes. And yes, you will receive a copy of the audio if you want one. You will also automatically receive a copy of the transcript by email to your personal email address.

Firstly – thank you for attending this appointment – not a lot of people bother with their exit interview.

'Yeah sorry, Michael,' they say. 'I was planning to come to my exit interview, but I'm just not able to make it now for some reason. I'm sure you'll be glad to get that hour back,' they say.

I understand, I tell them. Of course, I say that I understand. Don't worry. There's not much else you can say.

They apologise, but also, they act like it's not really a big deal. 'Yeah, sorry,' they say. 'Yeah, sorry! What's the point though? It's over. I've gone. Yeah, sorry.'

'Don't worry,' I tell them.

I've never been a brave man. I'm not brave enough to explain to them that an exit interview is not about anyone gaining something. Nobody immediately gets anything. It's just *a good thing to do*. A finality. But I don't ever say it. We don't do this good thing.

'Don't worry.'

How sad.

They go out through the door and are completely free. It's just some butterflies. It was never a person. That's what I tell myself when they cancel the exit interview. I use the time to do my breathing exercises in the meeting room, or in my shoffice if I

am at home. I make a note about it in my journal. I include
them in my thoughts. They are beautiful exotic birds, I say to
myself. Or, you know, whatever represents freedom on that
particular day. Like air. And they're gone and I forget their
names almost instantly. I forget their shape. It's sad really, and beautiful. Evaporation.

But *you* have not yet evaporated. *You* are here. And this is so
much more meaningful than being a bird or a butterfly. You are a
person!

So, to clarify, this interview is not some last-minute plea to get
you to stay. We are all on board with your decision. We will cope.
It's fine! You've no idea how fine it is. You're missing out on an
exciting new phase here, but that's no longer your concern. We are
glad for you. *I am glad for you.*

I remember feeling very glad inside, and thinking how good it
is to be young and to be able to make such sudden and completely
impulsive decisions.

I know you had a leaving party, and a lot of people attended.
That's normal, completely normal to celebrate your time here –
everyone wants to give you a send-off. You will always be one of
the family, that's what they're saying by attending your party. A
sign of lasting admiration and respect.

I am so sorry I was unable to make it. You enjoyed yourself, I
heard. You had a good time, by all accounts. Everyone says so.

I was unavoidably delayed at home on the night of your leaving
party. My dog – did you ever meet my dog? Perhaps it shambled
into view when we were on a call or something. I never brought
it to the office, my dog. I think the ambient fragrance they use on
our floor would drive it completely insane.

Anyway, that night I could not come out because my dog savaged something. And I mean, it absolutely tore another animal to
pieces. It was a bloody mess, if I can be honest with you. We don't
know what was savaged. It could have been anything. I mean, right

up to even a cow it could have been. I'm not joking. A cow, no problem. Can you imagine? Absolutely everywhere there was a horrible mess and the smell was unspeakable.

Very little of the animal was left intact, which led to some very idiotic speculation from my neighbour.

Let me tell you about my neighbour. We have to call him Glen, because that's his name. Glen from next door. He came to my house in his dressing gown and his slippers holding bits of this bloody mess in a newspaper. 'Look what your dog did! Look what your dog did!' he's saying – holding it out to me like it's fish and chips. 'This is only a sample!' he said. Oh, on and on he went.

He came through, into my kitchen, where I was very busy with something. Could have been that I was busy with something private, but that doesn't stop Glen. Privacy means nothing to him. He marched through my house, shoes on.

Well, so OK, not shoes, but slippers. Slippers, OK, granted, not shoes.

But he had been in the street with them, near that bloody mauled mess, so really the slippers become shoes at that point. In his dirty shoes, and dumped this mess on the kitchen counter. I couldn't deny it was probably my dog that had caused it to happen. Sometimes my dog gets an idea in its head and it just follows through with it, no matter how stupid or destructive. It sees a cow or a horse or a bear – it could have been a young or weakened bear. Maybe just a bear that was not at its best. It could have been a bear. My dog wouldn't shy away from a bear anyway, is what I mean.

You look incredulous. I'd advise you to remove that look from your facial vocabulary – going forward, it won't help you out there. My dog has definitely molested and wounded a young bear at least once in its life. People don't believe me but it's true.

The police officer who came over later tried to get us all to accept that the remains could have been a portion of fox, but nobody was really satisfied with this idea. Even Glen conceded that it could have been a portion of fox. Although he was now going in the opposite direction, size-wise.

From the beginning, my neighbour was convinced that the victim of the savaging had been his cat. He's got no idea. A cat's body, even badly mauled, does not look like this. Even spread out as thin as butter, it wouldn't cover anything like the same amount of space. There would be limited amounts of *stuff*, right? This was not a cat. It was totally the wrong size. Something else has happened to that cat.

The police officer concurred; absolutely the wrong size, he said. Very unlikely to be a cat.

I'll get to the point in a minute, this is all related. Exit interviews can take a few swerves before we arrive at the point – interconnectedness, yes? You are leaving here, but arriving somewhere, aha, else. Nothing is ever a true ending. So . . .

Very unlikely to be a cat. Those were the words of the police officer. I'm calling that a legal position, since a police officer said it. Legally, it wasn't a cat. That's my view – and I told Glen as much. So if he tries to take me to court, I will be able to say that it has been stated, legally stated, that this dead animal was not a cat. Legally not a cat, basically.

What do you think? Would you call that a fair position? Legally not a cat?

I'm asking seriously. You're normally so assertive with your views, you see? I am keen to hear. Normally, we hear from you even when the subject is not connected to your normal duties.

In addition, if it helps you make up your mind, I can assert, without any doubt whatsoever, that my dog would not hurt Glen's cat. My dog has nothing but respect for Glen's cat. My dog believes that cat to be one of the most dignified beings on planet Earth, if you want my honest appraisal.

I will confine my remarks on this issue now. We are veering away, even for a loosely agenda'd meeting like an exit interview. Point is, I missed your leaving party and I felt terrible. I made you this card. Can you see? I have been doing a course in watercolour landscapes online.

I've done a lot of online courses recently, as you know.

I did one on paper weaving a few months ago, perhaps I told you, but probably not. I have to say I paper-weaved a lot of things before I realised it's not for me. I paper-weaved a lot of bowls and lacquered them and painted them and put fruit in them and put them all around the house. It began to look somewhat obsessive.

The last one I made, I gave to my sister. I hadn't planned on making them for anyone else, especially family, because it causes such tension to hand-make something that will be on public display in a family member's house. What if they despise it! And then they have to walk past it every day, and either make themselves ignore it, or actively curse its existence. And in so doing, curse your existence. Big mistake, hand-making stuff for family. John Lewis gift card, box of chocs, leave it at that. But I did make one for my sister, as I said, a fruit bowl, because her husband had smashed their old fruit bowl.

He came home late one night and it ended up smashed, that's what she told me.

Tired from work, was the official line. Didn't want to put the lights on apparently. In case he woke someone. And then, I suppose, in the dark, he managed to stumble or something, and reach into the far, oblique end of the peninsular work surface, and, with quite a natural movement, accidentally lift, and then drop the china fruit bowl against the opposite wall, where the mildewed easy peeler printed itself onto the wall clock.

So I didn't say anything, but while I listened to this story of how the fruit bowl, one of the last pieces of the crockery set from our parents' wedding, came to be shattered, I began mentally paper-weaving them an unshatterable fruit bowl. Something more flexible for their highly volatile kitchen layout.

I presented it a few weeks later. The husband didn't even say thank you. He tucked his jumper into his trousers and went out somewhere. We don't get on.

So, paper-weaving, no. Not any longer. But watercolour landscapes, very much yes. I don't talk about it at work, any of this. My family, my hobbies. I don't talk about much at work at all, really. Have you noticed? I don't want to burden you, my direct reports, with my problems or my sad little hobbies.

None of us really share, do we, is my point. Do you see? This is a theme of our exit interview, I believe: 'communication'. At least, I feel sure it should be. We don't share enough, as a team. Or at least, nobody shares with me. Which is fine. I'm the manager, I have to accept these things. You don't want a manager dragging his midnight brother-in-law into the sprint-planning meeting. Or the weird things my dog does. Oh, there have been lots of things I have never communicated effectively about my dog.

'I was in the kitchen this morning,' I have never said, 'and the dog licked my foot, so I moved my foot away, and the dog continued to try and lick me, following me around, harassing me, trying to lick my foot, I couldn't get it to stop, so I had to shut myself in the bathroom.'

I never say this kind of thing at work, but it happens to me all the time. Of course, I have found it OK to be in the bathroom in the morning because eventually I have to go in there at some point anyway and have my shower and everything, but often the dog is doing this at a time when I am not at all ready. I stay in the bathroom and remind myself that it was my idea to get a dog.

I never say this at work. And thank god. I don't think you would have stayed even as long as you have if I mentioned to you that I have spent well over an hour in the bathroom most mornings with no practical purpose at all. My skin is over-moisturised.

This is an official view from a confirmed skin specialist. I have moved a lot of my belongings into the bathroom. I never talk about this, but I have a small library in there now, and I have an extension lead running under the door. Incredibly dangerous, but there it is. This is not every day — the foot-licking from my dog. Often the licking and harassing doesn't happen, and we enjoy a normal human–dog relationship. But on other days, it does happen. Do you think you would have stayed with us longer if I had come in every morning and explained that I am completely drained because my dog abusively licks my feet? No. Of course not. Your new employer's luxury approach to holiday allowance and remote working and the fifteen-per-cent pay bump would still have tempted you away. Your growing stature and courageous approach to life decisions would have disregarded my problems completely. As is right, of course. I'm not saying you would have been wrong to leave if you knew I spent most mornings telling you that I'm totally worn out. Exhausted emotionally as well as physically by this foot situation with my dog. My dog whom I love.

Physically exhausted? Yes, because I get no sleep on the days when this takes place. I'd say that for every foot-licking event, there are three nights of sleep completely lost, and a further four nights partially interrupted. You are good at maths, so you can already see that I'm losing a week of proper sleep every time the foot-licking event occurs, and it is more or less a biweekly thing.

So that's an example of something I don't talk about at work. I'm sure you have your own private things that you don't discuss in the office. If I had been at your leaving drinks you might have told me something, I suppose, about your life. I wouldn't have pried, I don't pry. I wouldn't have mentioned it at all, but we'd have ended up there. I'm bad at small talk, especially when there is alcohol involved. I tend to overshare. Something about the sound the heating makes in your rented accommodation, in the middle of the night, you might have been more willing to discuss things of that nature. You might have described your terror in the night. Or how you occasionally find yourself floating on air when the sun hits the dining room window at the right time of day, and you forget yourself, leave your body, and go as a dust mote into the proton beams of the sun. Or maybe you play chess or something.

You can see the picture I made for you features a field that has been converted into allotments. The date of the conversion was around 1986, which is not what I had expected when I enquired to the allotment committee. I had been expecting wartime. Dig for victory. But no, apparently the land was bought by the council in 1984 and then turned into an allotment a couple of years later thanks to a local community group petition.

There are many allotments, as you can see – this is a view I have considered beautiful for many years. And, in this picture, I felt sure you would enjoy the way I have accentuated the gridlike nature of the plots. The way they are divided up like a spreadsheet. Here is someone fiddling in their pumpkin area. Here is someone enjoying a sandwich. This here, this is the happy woman – everyone knows about her. There was a feature about her in the allotment newsletter – which I read avidly, despite having no interest in actually cultivating an allotment – she is there having a sip of gin from a tin. She is just in heaven, the newsletter says, as soon as she sets foot on these allotments. The world fades away, she says, there is nothing at all to consider beyond those brambles and hedges. She talks about the overwhelming sense of peace that she experiences there. She says she feels unburdened by the bad years of her life when she is on her allotment. Heavy years, she calls them, which are lifted away – the things in those years, the damage they inflicted – have never happened at all in her allotment.

There she is, just there – I have given her a Minnie Mouse sweatshirt. She never wears that kind of thing. I don't think she is that kind of person at all, but I felt the impulse to add a Minnie Mouse to her jumper. I'm sure I have artistic license to add this – I don't think you will get any calls from the lawyers of Walt Disney wishing to discuss the permissions associated with this image.

I go up there every day, and I do put some of my own thoughts and impressions onto the people. This man here, for example, is a known thief and is also a con artist. He does not have an allotment, but he goes there and will talk to people while they do their digging. He doesn't announce himself, but will appear there, and watch while people dig. His name is not known to me, but I call him Horville. It's not a real name.

There are dozens of figures in here, in this picture I made for you as a leaving gift. Dozens of living things. I will let you explore the rest of them.

This animal here is interesting! This one, do you see? I believe this is what my dog killed. I conducted some research this last week, and I'm convinced now that this is the animal I still have flecks of in my kitchen.

I'll be honest, I think this is a kind of sacred beast. A beast from a shrine maybe, in this man's plot, just here. He is called Steven, the man. Do you see this man here? This Steven? I believe this is the owner of the beast that was killed by my dog. I feel dreadful about it.

I met all the people I painted. I went down to the allotments from the hill where I was set up – and I asked everyone's permission to paint them and their allotments. They mostly said yes without hesitation, especially when I showed them a sketch – the sketch was very similar to the finished object you now hold in your hands (actually that you have placed face down on the meeting room table). They could see from the sketches that I was representing them as the most basic figures imaginable. It could be them, but it could easily be anyone else. I refer you to Minnie Mouse once again – can you tell it's her? Impossible to tell. Impossible. She didn't mind me adding that detail, the happy woman, she didn't really care at all – she just told me to do what I love and be happy. We had a gin together. It was a nice afternoon. But this guy, this Steven, he did not want me to represent him. So this figure here, this is not at all what the real Steven looks like. Out of respect for him, I made every effort to disguise his physical appearance in this stick figure here.

His allotment is a shrine. I realise on the page it is simply a dark smudge that, yes, for some reason is hot to the touch, and yes it also causes that odd sensation, doesn't it? The sensation when you touch Steven's scorched plot that several hundred appalling memories are coming back to you at once. I experienced it very strongly just now when I pointed him out to you. Do you have a Twix? I know you sometimes have a Twix with you in that shoulder bag you are famous for carrying. Can you please give me a stick if you have a Twix? No Twix? OK, well fine. You should get something Twix-ish asap though.

I'm afraid that, as part of this exit interview, we are both going to have to touch Steven's shrine area again. I will go first.

And . . . there! Oh that was a bad one! Ouch! Oof!

I need a moment.

I don't know what you see when you touch this picture of Steven's allotment shrine, but what I see is this room that we are in now, and I cannot see anything else. Isn't that funny? It's a series of images, and in all of them it's still just this room that we are in now. I am in here with my aunt and I have not looked after her cat while she was away. I have allowed the cat to go hungry and remain locked in the house. I forgot, but the aunt is tremendously unforgiving. Then I am in here with a gas that represents the smell of gas in the caravan we used to stay in on holiday in Wales with the Bennetts. And the Bennetts caravan was a happy place, and our caravan was a cold place. Then I am rotating in deep space but also, I am still in this room. There seems to be no way of leaving the room and entering space itself, but the room is in space. I am in space in this room.

All this because of Steven's allotment.

His allotment is a shrine but I have no idea what it is a shrine to. There is a stone object there, in the centre of the smudge.

In reality this stone object is an enormous beast-like totem. So totemic and vast in fact, that I cannot describe its features accurately. It looked incredibly real, for something that has no business existing, that is.

He calls it Smerminon, Simon does.

'Smerminon is harmless,' Steven told me when I went to ask if I could put him in my picture. 'But I wouldn't risk it. I don't even look directly at him most days,' Steven told me.

'Well,' I said to him, 'I think Smerminon is quite marvellous. I'd love to include his likeness in my picture. It's for a leaving present for a valued colleague,' I told him.

While I was explaining all this, Steven was watching me with a look of amused puzzlement on his face. It was as though he had never been asked before if he could be painted as part of a land-scape. I tried again.

'I am likely to miss the leaving party of this colleague, you see? They will be upset I think, so I want to give them something special and I thought a picture of the allotment would be most fitting.' I told him, quite open and honestly.

We got into a whole muddle where he started calling me an artist and saying he didn't like artists. Something about his friend falling in with some artists many years ago, and getting a cocaine addiction.

I told him I was not that kind of artist, but simply an amateur who liked to do courses and apply what I have learnt to making gifts for significant people in my life.

'I'd love to paint you and your fascinating plot,' I said. 'From a distance of course. Look, here is the sketch I made earlier.'

Steven did not like the sketch, he burned it. He was very polite about burning it, but he did burn it.

'Sorry,' he said. 'I have to burn this now. Smerminon will be terribly upset if I allow an unofficial likeness to be created. I hope you understand.'

While he was being polite like this, Steven had snatched my sketch book away from me and was roughly riffling through it, looking for more sketches that might have shown his beloved Smerminon. He ruined several promising views of Fournier Bay, which is in Cornwall. Simply miles away from this allotment. A real shame.

Anyway, this whole thing with Steven was disturbing and I wanted to end it as quickly as I could, so I agreed to depict him as a completely generic stick figure who, if it looks like anyone, looks like Charles Dance the actor. I agreed also to redact the image of his plot. It would be represented as a redaction. Something is there, but nothing that can be depicted.

So anyway, long story short, that statue of Smerminon probably came to life one night and tangled with my dog, and my dog mauled it to death.

Can you understand now why I wasn't there with you at your leaving party? I wanted to be there. I wanted nothing more than to be able to relax and open up a bit, and just wish you all the luck in the world in your new role, because you absolutely deserve it. You really do deserve all the luck in the world. They are so lucky to have you. So I suppose they also have a lot of luck on their side.

I don't know if this appeals to you at all, but I did actually manage to get a few cuts of the meat that was not my neighbour's cat, and was probably Smerminon. I put it in these sandwiches just here. I thought this could be our final lunch together. It tastes just like salt beef. I did actually add a lot of salt to it. Also mustard, double cream, some home-made vegetable stock, black pepper, tarragon, and tomato ketchup (which I admit was a mistake – I was trying to be far too clever there).

I think this is why you really ought to have brought a Twix. I was sort of banking on that because it would round this off nicely. But you haven't. It's fine that you haven't.

I'd love to hear your thoughts on all this. This is your interview after all. It's you who is leaving. Or actually, you are the one who has left. Although, of course, as you can see, you have not in fact managed to leave this room. You haven't moved a muscle in all this time.

Acknowledgements

Thank you always to my agent, Cathryn Summerhayes. To my editor Jason Arthur for trusting me and for his near-magical improvements to this work. To Sigrid Rausing for making Granta so much like home for me. To everyone who has worked with me at Curtis Brown and Granta – you are all the best.

Thanks always to my beautiful friends who are readers of my silly, often unfinished work:

Dan Roberts, Charlie Tittle, Bryn Tittle, Emma Bennett, Holly Pester, Tim MacGabhann, Claire Carroll, Tom Conaghan, Emma Wright, Luke Kennard, Jack Underwood.

I want to thank all the editors who have worked with me on earlier versions of these stories, and allowed me space to experiment:

Luke Neima, Guillermo Stitch, Dan Crowe, Lucy Binnersly, Andrea Mason, Dominic Jaeckle, Hann Clarke, Gary Kaill and Henry Johns.

Thanks specifically to Cosima Fournet-Pester, for first explaining to me about Sail Away Land, and for lending me this name.

Thank you to Emilie, Orson and Coco who give meaning to this and all worlds.